THE MERVIN GARDENS MURDERS

AN IZZY BRAND COMIC MYSTERY NOVELLA

by
IRV STERNBERG

D1565258

StarMount Press
Denver, Colorado

THE MERVIN GARDENS MURDERS

AN IZZY BRAND COMIC MYSTERY NOVELLA

by

IRV STERNBERG

The Mervin Gardens Murders
All Rights Reserved.
Copyright © 2020 Irv Sternberg

StarMount Press, Denver, CO 80247
ISBN: 9798679666320
Interior book design by Suzanne Proulx

Other books by Irv Sternberg

In the Land of the Morning Calm

The Ruby

Cobalt Blues

The Mayfly Murder

Death on the Not So Blue Danube

No Laughing Matter

Neptune's Chariot

Kilts and Knishes

WRITING AS MARK IRVING

The Persian Project

Sakura's Stratagem

Deadly Passage

Praise for previous books by Irv Sternberg

*Murder seems to follow aging comic Izzy Brand in this collection of three mystery novellas [*DEATH ON THE NOT-SO BLUE DANUBE*], whose protagonist is much like a modern-day Hercule Poirot. Readers are treated to Izzy's genuinely amusing stand-up comedy. Short but diverting whodunits featuring a laudable part-time detective.*

Kirkus Reviews

Stand-up comic Izzy Brand is an everyday sort of guy who could be your grandfather, favorite uncle or friendly neighbor but when he's not performing, dead bodies have a way of turning up wherever he goes. Sternberg is Agatha Christie with a sharp comic edge. (Izzy Brand mysteries.)

Margaret Coel, New York *Times* best-selling author

*Cheers to Irv Sternberg for giving us a female hero of such glowing courage. The things he describes in such convicting and large hearted way moved and amazed me. What a rip-roarer! (*NEPTUNE'S CHARIOT*)*

Joanne Greenberg, author of the classic *I Never Promised You A Rose Garden*

*Takes off with a jolt and doesn't touch down until it reveals the new dangers of international intrigue at the turn of the century. Mark Irving (pen name) writes his compelling page-turner with authority and confidence. (*SAKURA'S STRATAGEM*)*

Stephen White, New York *Times* best-selling author

Mark Irving keeps the tension crackling in his most ambitious novel. Fast-paced, provocative and populated with fascinating characters, SAKURA'S STRATAGEM *is a sure-fire winner.*

Michael Allegretto, author of *Grave Doubts*

For Jeanne, who came late into my life and added joyous years.

ONE

SIDNEY LUFT WAS NOT a vain man, but he allowed himself a modest measure of satisfaction at the thought that someone like Leah Lamont would find him attractive. After all, Leah, at the age of 64, was almost ten years younger than he. Moreover, she was almost as beautiful as she'd been while performing in movies, on the Broadway stage and on television. He'd just left her apartment where she prepared his favorite meal of a T-bone steak, pink in the middle, sweet potato and asparagus, sautéed not grilled. He'd brought a bottle of Saint Brendan's Irish Cream Liqueur for dessert. They sipped the cordial and chatted in the living room for a while before retiring to her exquisitely feminine bedroom with its pink bedding and pink drapes.

Because of rules she had established early in their relationship, he never stayed the night. After making love, he left her apartment about midnight, returning to his own in the same senior citizen luxury condo complex of five six-story buildings they shared with about 150 other residents in mid-town Denver. While her apartment was much larger than his—three bedrooms, a huge living room, dining room and a balcony, compared to his modest one-bedroom unit—he was comfortably settled after losing his wife to breast cancer eight years earlier. He had recently retired from his dentistry practice.

As he stepped from the shower, he caught a glimpse of himself in the mirror. At six feet-and-a fraction tall and weighing about 175 pounds, his body was relatively firm, having shed some fat during a recent strenuous regimen in the fitness center. And, unlike other men he knew of the same age, he had no problems making love. In his mind, he felt like he was in his fifties.

Luft put on his dark blue silk pajamas, a Christmas gift from Leah, and slipped into bed. For a few moments, he allowed his mind to mull over the day's events. They'd taken in a show which they agreed was worth seeing despite several negative reviews. Leah despised critics, often commenting on what she called "their pseudo-intellectual ranting." She often said she'd rather have a full house of appreciative attendees at her performances than a glowing review. Instead of dining downtown, she insisted they return to her apartment where she would prepare a late evening meal. How many women would do that? It was one of the many things about her that he greatly appreciated.

He'd been asleep for about an hour when he awoke, coughing. His chest felt tight. He had trouble breathing. The coughing continued so he got out of bed, went to the bathroom and drank a glass of water. He felt hot. He was sweating and felt nauseated. He splashed a handful of cold water over his face and felt some relief. He returned to bed and tried to fall asleep.

A few minutes later, he had a violent coughing fit. He sat upright and clenched his throat. He couldn't breathe. He gasped for air, and then fell back, his head on the pillow in a skewed position, his bulging eyes open, seeing nothing.

TWO

Anita and I were having a leisurely lunch at a rustic restaurant in the foothills west of Denver when her cell rang. I disliked allowing a phone call to interrupt a dining experience, but I understood her need to answer. As a psychotherapist with sometimes needy patients, she let them know she was always available. I heard her say, "We'll be right there." Placing her cell back into her purse, she said, "Leah's gentleman friend was just found dead in his apartment."

"Sidney?" I blurted. "We just saw him the other night. What happened?"

"I don't know. But he's the fifth person to die in Leah's building this year. She thinks they've all been murdered, and she's scared to death. I told her we're coming over."

From the tone of her voice and the set of her jaw, I knew our lunch was over before I could enjoy the slice of double chocolate cake the server had just placed on the table. I also knew there would be no point in resisting. Leah and Anita were close friends and any resistance I suggested would be quickly dismissed by my devoted companion. Nevertheless, I made an attempt.

"Let me give Carlos a call," I said, referring to Denver Detective Carlos Collins, my friend on the Denver Police Department. "I'd like to know what the official police report is on those other deaths Leah is talking about."

Anita made a wry expression. "That's not the point, Izzy. She's frightened and needs some comforting right now. Let's go."

"Maybe Sidney had a heart attack," I said. "Sometimes that happens to men of a certain age when they're having sex."

"Izzy, this is no time for jokes"

"I wasn't joking. It's a fact. That's why I try to take care of my heart."

Anita looked at me. "Are you serious? If *that's* really a concern, we could—"

"Never mind," I said, regretting I'd said anything.

I paid the check and we were off to Mervin Gardens, the condo where Leah lived. There are some who believe the builder wanted to name his project *Marvin* Gardens because he enjoyed playing Monopoly, but was persuaded by his attorney to change it to avoid a possible copyright infringement suit. Others said the builder chose Mervin Gardens because, after years of trying, his wife finally gave birth to a boy they promptly named Mervin. The large complex had a reputation for being a safe, comfortable place to live for its 55-and-over affluent and mostly active residents. They had about fifteen clubs and activities to choose from to occupy their time. It seemed to be a happy community.

On the drive to Leah's place I said, "Leah sounds a bit hysterical."

"She's not the type to be hysterical, Izzy. And just because she's a retired actress doesn't mean she's prone to be dramatic. She's very level-headed and objective."

I reviewed what I knew about her long-time friend. Leah Lamont was still attractive, alert, and an engaging conversationalist. I could understand why Sidney Luft, a widower, would want her company, even at their advanced ages. Since I'm in my eighties, I know the demands of my own heart and what makes it flutter occasionally—thanks to Anita. I'm a part-time stand-up comic but I try to spend as much time with her as possible. We have a chemistry that has added years to my life. That's why I adore her. We've known each other for about ten years. I'd marry her in a heartbeat. I've asked her several times, but she's always said 'no' because she was still getting over a bad marriage. I'm an optimist. I'll keep asking.

When I'm not performing at my downtown comedy club, I've also picked up another activity. I've been solving murders in recent years with Anita's help. It's not that I was looking for a new career as a homicide detective as my late wife sometimes teases me in my dreams. It just seems that wherever I go I seem to stumble over bodies. So I wind up getting involved.

We were out of the foothills and entering the stream of traffic in Denver's busy highways and boulevards. It had been a mild winter and now in late spring the trees around the Civic Center were beginning to bud and a rainbow of colorful flowers dotted the landscapes in front of City Hall. I resisted the temptation to gawk, reminding myself that people of my age often have accidents while driving because they are daydreaming. *Pay attention to your driving, Izzy!*

For years Denver was just a "dusty old cow town" as one of the local columnists frequently called it, but in recent years the city attracted hordes of newcomers, drawn by a bustling economy, great weather and, of course, the scenery. You could play golf in the morning and go skiing in the afternoon. "'Tis a privilege to live in Colorado," the local paper proclaimed on its editorial page. I agreed. However, housing was an issue. The cost of new homes and apartment rentals was among the nation's highest. I wondered how ordinary people could afford them. And then I read about the salaries some young people were earning— $200,000 a year, or more, mostly in the growing tech industry which rivaled California's. In fact, some called the metro Denver area "Colorado's Silicon Valley." Of course, not everyone made that kind of money. Some newcomers found it was simply too expensive to live here, so they moved, either returning to their former locations or heading elsewhere where the cost of living was lower.

After a 40-minute drive we arrived at the entrance to Mervin Gardens. A large alabaster statue of a young nude couple embracing each other stood on a pedestal. The developers had commissioned the work as a piece of art, but some residents objected. The developers covered the statue with a shroud. It remained hidden from sight for years. Changing times and more liberal-minded residents persuaded the Home Owners Association's board of directors to remove the shroud. Leah told us that hardly anyone paid any attention to it anymore. Nor do they mind that the complex was called "Menopause Manor" and similar sobriquets in years past.

The quartet of identical buildings formed a circle around a two-story administrative building that housed the business office, a few meeting rooms, an auditorium, restaurant and a tennis shop. Nearby were the tennis courts, a horseshoe lane, an outdoor swimming pool and a large gazebo to shelter picnic tables and chairs. All were located on a large, immaculately-groomed green belt, festooned with colorful flower beds and shrubs.

Mature trees provided sporadic shaded areas

I parked in the large parking area in front of Leah's building and walked the concrete path to the front entrance. The six-story building held four apartments on each floor and faced a large common area of magnificent trees and dense shrubbery. In the summer, colorful flower beds bloomed almost like a botanical garden. It was like walking through a park.

In the lobby, Leah buzzed us in. She greeted us in the doorway of her elegantly furnished apartment on the second floor. Upon seeing Anita, Leah fell into her arms and immediately began crying. Anita said, "I'm so sorry. He was a good man." Leah cried harder.

Without asking, I knew why Leah had called Anita. It wasn't just because they were good friends, almost like sisters, but because Leah knew that I had solved a few murders in recent years. Not that pursuing homicides had become my profession. It started when my best friend, Sam Goodman, was found beaten to death in a LoDo alley near his office. Police had charged a homeless man, but I was able to prove the killer was someone else.

Since then it seems that bodies kept showing up wherever I went and, well, somehow I got involved. Now, I had the same feeling in Leah's apartment— that I would be investigating Sidney's death.

Seated in an arm chair, I started asking questions and, between sobs, Leah offered answers.

"We had dinner here," she murmured. "He likes ... he *liked* my steak and potatoes. He helped clear the table and put the dishes in the dishwasher. He was feeling fine. We went into the living room and sat on the sofa."

"And then what?" I asked.

Leah gave me a look that would freeze an Eskimo's testicles. "If I wanted you to know I would tell you."

Anita made a peculiar noise that sounded like she was stifling a laugh. I re-positioned myself in my chair.

"I meant after he left," I said, attempting to regain my composure.

Leah folded her hands in her lap. "I fell asleep. Apparently he went to bed in his apartment, too, because when I couldn't reach him this morning, I called our Security Patrol. They entered his apartment about 10 a.m. and found him still in bed in his pajamas. He was . . . dead." She began crying again.

I went to the sofa where she was sitting, sat beside her and put an arm around her. "I'm sorry, Leah."

She put her head on my shoulder and cried louder. I felt badly for her. I know what it's like to lose a loved one. My wife, Clara, died almost 50 years ago and I still have warm memories of our brief years together. My life was very lonely until I met Anita. She brought joy back into my life. I can't believe I'm still around. I think she's the reason why.

"What did the Security Patrol do?" I asked her gently, even though I knew her probable response.

She sat up and folded her hands again. "They called for an ambulance. Then the Denver police arrived and asked me some questions. I understand the medical examiner examined the body. My friends and neighbors here have already started calling. They're assuming Sidney died of natural causes like the others, but I don't believe it. I don't believe any of them died naturally. I think they were *all* murdered." She hesitated before adding, "and I think the police will consider me a suspect because I may have been the last person to see him alive. Oh, Izzy, what shall I do?"

THREE

THE DRIVE TO ANITA'S cozy townhome in upscale Cherry Creek North took only about twenty minutes. As we passed through the tony commercial district off First Avenue, she made her pitch. "Whether she's right or not, Izzy, you must look into this. Even if it's only to calm her. I know her not only as a friend but as a client. Trust me, Leah really needs you to investigate."

"You know the odds aren't very good that she's right. Which means she's not a suspect."

"I know, Izzy, but please do your best to placate her. She's a real dear. I hate to see her so upset." She placed a hand on my knee.

"Do you do that with your male clients?" I teased.

"Do what?"

I looked down at her hand.

"Pay attention to your driving," she said, and withdrew her hand.

A few minutes later we were at her townhouse. At her door, she said, "Are you coming in?"

14

"I think I'll drop in on Carlos. If I'm going to check out Leah's suspicions, I should learn what the Denver PD has to say about these deaths. And maybe I can assure her that the cops won't be investigating her."

"That would be a relief. Are we still on for dinner before your show tomorrow night?"

"I'll pick you up at 5 o'clock." She kissed me before disappearing into her house.

***

Carlos Collins, my friend at the Denver PD, had a Mexican mother and an Irish father. I remember him as a little boy, running down the hall of the apartment house near Denver's West Side, where his grandparents lived. My late wife, Clara, and I were a newly married couple when we moved in next door to them. Carlos's grandparents befriended us and invited us to home-cooked Mexican dinners. We played with the boy quite a bit and grew fond of him. His parents and grandparents consoled me when Clara died during childbirth. The baby, a little girl, also died. For a long time I was very angry at the doctor and the hospital. Sam Goodman, my best friend, helped me grieve. So did Carlos' grandparents.

I watched with pride as Carlos grew up, won varsity letters playing football and basketball at North High School and football at the Colorado State University in Fort Collins. His dad joked they named the city after his family. I attended his graduation, and then saw him join the Denver Police Department and rise steadily through the ranks to detective. Because I occasionally solved murders, we developed a different kind of relationship. At first he was annoyed that I was poking around in police business, but eventually I earned his respect for my amateur sleuthing. These days he even offers advice and gives me tips. Sometimes it's hard for me to believe the little boy who chased a ball down the hall is now a respected detective, a married man and a soon-to-be-father.

He was seated at his desk on the second floor of the Denver PD headquarters building on Cherokee Street in downtown Denver when I greeted him. *"Buenos días, señor capitán,"* I said. Ever since he joined the Denver PD, I always addressed him by a rank or two above his grade.

"Hey, Izzy, how you doin'?"

"Great, Carlos. How's Erin?" His wife was due with their first baby in about a month.

"Man, she's developed peculiar eating tastes. Dill pickles and ice cream. At 1 a.m. Do pregnant woman always do that? Is that normal?"

"Sounds familiar, kid." Even though he was nearing thirty, I still called him *kid*. "I think Clara had an appetite for some peculiar stuff while she was carrying. So is it a boy or a girl?"

"We don't know. Haven't tried to find out. We want to be surprised."

"Good. That's the old-fashioned way. There's no reason you need to know in advance."

"Well, it would give us a head start on decorating the baby's room and picking out some clothes. You know—pink or blue?"

I chuckled. "You'll sort it out, don't worry."

"So what brings you downtown, Izzy?"

"Do you know Anita's friend, Leah Lamont, the retired actress?

"Yeah, she's still a good-looking babe."

"Her gentlemen friend just died. Do you have the coroner's report?"

Carlos swiveled his chair and sent a skeptical look my way. "Izzy, whenever you ask me about a coroner's report it means you're snooping around. What is it this time?"

"Leah thinks her guy was murdered. In fact, she thinks there's been a string of murders in the condo where she lives. Anita wants me to take a look."

I'm pretty sure I heard Carlos sigh, his way of signaling skepticism and impatience. He does that almost automatically whenever I approach him with a suggestion that everything is not kosher.

"What's his name?"

"Sidney Luft. He was found dead in his bed."

"Address?"

I pulled a small notebook from my pocket and flipped pages until I found the information Carlos wanted. The habit of carrying a notebook was something I picked up from Carlos on my first homicide investigation. Watching Carlos at work was like taking a cram course in police procedures. I tried copying his routine. I gave him the street address of the Mervin Gardens complex and Sidney's apartment number. "He lived on the third floor."

"What about those other deaths? Do you have names and addresses?"

I shook my head. "All I know about them is that they all lived in the same building that Leah lives in. And that all the deaths occurred this year."

"Sex?"

"At their ages, I doubt it."

Carlos sighed again.

"Two men, three women," I said. "Leah said they all lived alone."

Carlos punched a key on his cell phone and express-dialed a number. "Hi, Thelma. It's Carlos. Can you tell me what you've got on a Sidney Luft at the Mervin Gardens complex?" He put his phone on speaker mode while he waited, presumably so that I could hear her response. "Coroner's office," he told me. After a moment Thelma came back and said, "Cardiac arrest. Nothing suspicious."

"Thanks, Thelma. I understand you had other deaths at the same place earlier this year. Nothing came across my desk, so can I assume they also were natural causes?"

"Actually, we've had four deaths there so far

this year. Luft will make it five. And, yes, all were natural. It's to be expected at a place like that. Nothing unusual."

"Thanks, again, sweetheart."

"You're welcome. Say 'hi' to Erin."

Carlos turned off his cell and faced me. "Anything else, Izzy?"

"So there's no chance of starting an investigation?" I asked. "There's no homicide case here?"

"None," he insisted.

"That's what I thought. Now I've got to convince Leah she has nothing to worry about. She's afraid she'd be a suspect."

"At least you don't have to deal with another homicide, or five."

As I left Denver PD, Carlos' last words comforted me because I had a gig scheduled tomorrow night at the club and the last thing I needed was a distraction like murder, or multiple murders. I pushed the thought from my mind and started focusing on my routine. After a quick supper of franks and beans, I called Anita and Leah and told them what Carlos had said. Then I took George for a walk around the block of my condo in the area they call the Golden Triangle. George is my one-eyed farting Boston terrier. He was a stray when I found him. I think he lost an eye in a fight with a cat. He also has an intestinal problem that causes him to release lots of gas. But he's a good companion and puts up with my faults, too, so we're even. We watched some TV together before going to bed.

***

I don't like to eat a big meal before my show, so I took Anita to the Brooklyn Deli on Hampden and ordered a bowl of chicken soup with a matzo ball. Anita had a corned beef sandwich on dark rye and a side of coleslaw. The place was packed for the Early Bird special which they started serving at 4:30. We were there forty-five minutes later. I saw a familiar face seated at a nearby table. We made eye contact and I rose and walked to his table. He had recently put his wife in a nursing home for Alzheimer patients after more than fifty years of marriage. He was a likeable guy, and I felt sad for him. I was glad to see him dining out, even if he was alone.

"Hello, Izzy, nice to see you," he said. "Long

time. Where've you been?"

"Anita and I took a trip around the world, Larry. Next year we're going somewhere else."

It took a few seconds for the joke to register. Then the light went on. He laughed. "Always performing, Izzy. That's you! Always on stage."

I hate to see people eating by themselves. It always seemed to me a sad scene. "Hey, Larry, come join us." I gripped his elbow and helped him up. "Honey, remember Larry Slater? We met him at a Marine Corps veterans' party last year. I asked him to join us."

He looked at Anita. "Do you mind?"

"Not at all," she said, pointing to an empty chair. "Please."

I don't often invite people to join us, so for that reason I knew Anita wouldn't mind. If you can't be kind to a lonely old man who just put his wife in a nursing home, when *are* you going to be? Larry sat down and we engaged him in conversation. I knew he loved baseball, so we talked about the Rockies, the high expectations we had for them the previous years, and the disappointments we suffered. When the pitching was good, the hitting stunk. And when the batters were hot, the pitchers went cold. It was enough to drive you nuts.

"I can't believe we almost finished in last place," I grumbled.

"Wait 'til next year," Larry said.

"You sound like an old Brooklyn Dodgers fan," I said.

He grinned. "I used to be. Those were the good old days. Rooting for the old Dodgers taught you to be an optimist. Here we are years later, and I see the same thing happening with Rockies' fans. We're learning how to look forward to next year."

"So how's business?" I asked him. He owned a small medical supply firm.

"Business is good. People are always getting sick, thank goodness." He chuckled at his own dark humor. But that made him think of his wife, and his demeanor changed.

"How is Shirley doing?" I asked.

His face crumpled with pain. "Not good," he murmured. "She's going downhill very fast."

"We're sorry," I said, as Anita reached across the table and gently patted his hand. "Is there anything we can do?" she asked.

He smiled weekly. "I'm afraid not, but thanks for asking. It's just a matter of time. I don't know what I'll do when she's gone."

Dinner over, he clasped my hand and shook it. "You're a real *mensch,* Izzy. It's been a privilege to know you."

On the way to the club for my performance, Anita said, "That was a real compliment that he paid you, Izzy. Not everyone is called a *mensch.*"

"I know, honey, but I'm thinking about the *other* thing he said."

"You mean that 'it's been a privilege to know you'?"

"Yes. It was like he was saying 'goodbye.'"

***

They call the place "The Izzy Brand Comedy Club" but I don't own it. The owner is Danny Goodman, son of the late Sam Goodman. Sam and I grew up together on Denver's West Side, graduated from North High, enlisted in the Marines and served in Korea. One bitter-cold night when the sky was pitch black, a Chinese soldier sneaked into our lines and was about to shove a bayonet into my back. Sam saw him and shot him in the head with his .45 Colt. The war over, we returned to Colorado and enrolled at the University of Colorado in Boulder. Sam majored in business administration, I majored in goofing off. I barely got through my classes—English, history, psychology—but spent two years on top of my class in clowning around. Telling jokes was my preoccupation. Getting laughs was my goal. I drove my professors crazy.

I left CU in my junior year to try my hand at comedy. I played all the really small clubs for peanuts a gig. Every performance taught me something new. I learned how to handle all kinds of audiences. I sharpened my routine. I began to attract attention, played bigger clubs, drew larger audiences, earned more money and hired an agent. I even hired a guy to write some jokes for me. Then Ed Sullivan's people called my agent. I was about to become big-time. On the night I performed on Ed's show, he had another "nobody" on stage—a kid named Elvis Presley. When it was over, hardly anyone even remembered me being on the show.

Meanwhile, my friend Sam Goodman was doing

very well in business. He became a developer. He gained a reputation for building substantial homes and classy commercial buildings. He had an office on the edge of the Lower Downtown area, a downtrodden neighborhood of boarded-up warehouses, flop houses and saloons. The streets were littered with homeless people and winos. One night police found Sam's badly beaten body in an alleyway in LoDo. Police said it was an apparent mugging and theft. The police arrested a homeless man.

By now, Carlos Collins was a rookie detective. It was his case, and he was convinced he had the right man. But I was skeptical. That's why I decided to investigate on my own. My hunch was right. In the end I learned that the killer mistook Sam for someone else. I was glad that I could find closure for Sam and his family. And I was glad that my work freed an innocent man.

Danny inherited the comedy club and later named it after me in honor of my long friendship with his father. A wannabe standup himself, Danny is a good student and is eager to listen to the tips I frequently give him. In gratitude, he allows me to plan my own schedule at the club.

So, at my age, I perform only once a week—usually as the middler on Saturday night.

Tonight was Saturday night. I went into my routine.

Goldberg is standing in a long line at the supermarket, waiting to check out his groceries. He recognizes a Chinese neighbor in front of him. The cashier is slow and the line is moving about as fast as a teenager told to clean up his room. Goldberg grows impatient. He has other things to do. He feels his anger rising with no place to put it. Then he looks at the Chinese man and suddenly punches him in the back of his head.

"Hey," the Chinese man says, "What did you do that for, Goldberg?"

"Because you pulled a sneak attack on us at Pearl Harbor."

"No, I'm Chinese. That was the Japanese!"

Goldberg says: "Chinese, Burmese, Japanese, what's the difference? They're all the same!"

The Chinese man thinks about that for a moment and then punches Goldberg in the nose.

"Hey, what are you doing?" Goldberg complains.

"You sank the Titanic," the Chinese man says.

"No, it was an iceberg," Goldberg says.

"Iceberg, Rosenberg, Goldberg—what's the difference. They're all the same!"

FOUR

THE SHOW OVER, **I** took Anita home and she invited me inside for a nightcap. We sat next to each other on a loveseat, sipping our drinks and talking about the night's performance.

"Nice crowd tonight, "she said, "and they seemed to be enjoying themselves."

I agreed with her but I was also mindful that I was lucky. I heard there was an AARP convention earlier in the day so I had a ready-made audience for my routine. My jokes are aimed at older people and they filled the house tonight. Danny would be happy with the take. I was happy with their reception, although some of my gags came across as lame. It happens. On other nights the same jokes drew hearty laughs, tonight not so much. Every audience is different.

Some of the audience must have heard my jokes years ago, but that's what's nice about having a following of older people—they don't remember. So they laugh as if it's the first time they heard it, like the Goldberg and Chinaman story. I must've told that story at the club at least three or four times every year.

Our glasses were empty and Anita asked if I wanted another. I declined, having something else in mind. I slid closer to her and put an arm around her shoulder. She moved her head closer to mine. I stroked her hair, then traced her profile with my forefinger. I ran the finger down her forehead, and then down her *shiksa*-like nose to her lips. I ran my finger over her upper lip, then her bottom lip to her chin. I lifted her chin, leaned toward her and put my mouth gently on hers. She placed a hand behind my head and kissed me back. A few minutes later, we were in her bedroom, removing our clothes.

Young people often think it's incomprehensible that older people have sex. Some may even think it's repulsive imagining their *bubbies and zaidies* rolling around in bed, looking for the most comfortable position. The kids, as I call anyone under the age of fifty, have a lot to learn, and I hope they get the opportunity to find out for themselves. I'm mindful that many men my age are unable. For various reasons their equipment no longer works. That's true for women, too. But Anita and I are fortunate. We can arouse each other, make love slowly and passionately, and have climaxes. Our lovemaking is not the same as if we were 20-year-olds but it's just as satisfying, maybe even more so. Neither of us smokes so after making love we sipped some 2007 Cabernet Sauvignon I found in her kitchen cabinet.

"What did you learn from Carlos about the deaths at Mervin Gardens?" she asked.

"Nothing that would confirm Leah's suspicions."

"But don't you think it odd that five people living in the same building and all apparently in good health, according to Leah, would die within six months of each other?"

"Not necessarily, my sweet. They all lived long lives and were all at an age when their tickets start getting punched. Death is right around the corner for people who live in Mervin Gardens, and they know it. They even joke about it."

"Like who?"

"Well, I once heard Leah say that every time she hears an ambulance, she says to herself: 'there goes another condo for sale.'"

Anita chuckled. Then she turned serious. "You know, Izzy, there are 25 occupants in Leah's building. That means 20 percent of them died within five months. Even in a building occupied by old people, doesn't that statistic seem high?"

I'm not a numbers person—that's why I'm such a lousy poker player—but Anita's question seemed reasonable. Maybe I should take a peek into the situation. I could start by getting a list of all the residents in her building and learning as much about them as I can. I'd also ask Carlos to help me acquire the medical examiners' reports on all the deaths.

Wait a minute. This would be more than a peek. Sounds more like a full-blown investigation. Do I really want to do this?

Anita's question still hung in the air. She was waiting for me to respond. "I don't know much about statistics, honey, but that does seem like a high number."

"So what are you going to do?"

"I'll check around."

"Good! I'll tell Leah you're on the case. She'll be

so relieved. You already know a lot of people here, Leah and Sidney's gang at the pool. " They were a group of about seven or eight people, mostly women, who hung out at the outdoor pool all summer, sunning themselves and *schmoozing*. He and Anita occasionally joined them, as Leah's guests. They appeared to enjoy each other's company.

Oy vey, I said to myself. *Here I go again.* "Okay," I told Anita, "but Leah's got to help out. I need her to give me a list of all the other occupants in this building. I'm sure she has such a list."

"I'll call her first thing in the morning and get it for you."

"Good. While you're doing that I'll pay Carlos another visit. He'll be pissed. But right now I'd better go home. George is waiting for me to take him out."

***

Carlos was not pleased with my early morning request. I had asked him for a look at the official medical examiner reports on the five deaths. "Look, Izzy, I told you those deaths were attributed to natural causes. Why can't you simply accept that?"

"I know, I know. But what harm would it do to take another look at the reports? I promised Anita and Leah I would check it out. You wouldn't want me to tell them I couldn't keep my promise because a certain stubborn detective refused to cooperate, would you?"

The expression on Carlos's face was a mixture of incredulity and resignation. "Okay, Izzy, I'll get you those reports, but only because you're like part of the family. You are *mishapcha*."

"If you're going to speak Yiddish, at least speak it correctly. The word for family is *mishpacha*. I've solved three murders in recent years. How about that? Doesn't that earn me some creds?

Now the resignation part of his facial expression was in full control. "Yes, it does. But you need to know you're really pushing it. I'll get you those reports but I want them back on my desk within 24 hours."

***

The reports were like reading a checklist of medical terms that only professionals in the field could understand. In the end, they all amounted to the same thing: that by all indications, there was nothing to suggest the deaths were caused by anything unusual. Or, as Carlos would put it: case closed. But I knew Leah would not accept that conclusion, so where do I go from here?

I didn't have the patience to wrestle with that question right now. I was still thinking about my Saturday night gig. I needed to sharpen the routine. I needed some fresh material. I had a new joke that needed a tryout. Danny had a good ear and feel for comedy. He'll let me know right away if this one was marketable. I called him at the club.

"Okay, kid, what do you think of this?"

My doctor friend experienced his share of anti-Semitism when he tried to affiliate with one of the hospitals years ago in Denver. In those days there were no Jewish hospitals and Jewish physicians had real difficulty hooking up with a hospital. One day he was talking to some gentile doctors about his situation and one of them said:

Maybe you should try a different field, Morris. Most Jews I know play an instrument—a violin or piano, something. Maybe you should become a musician. What instrument do you play?

My friend, who is a gynecologist, said: I play the diaphragm.

Danny laughed out loud. "Yeah, that'll work, Izzy. I'd go with it. It's got a social message, too. But that other doctor is a shmuck."

FIVE

ATISFIED THAT MY NEW "diaphragm" joke would work, I sorted through my book of older successful jokes and chose enough to fill my gig for next Saturday, leaving room for anything new that might pop up before then. I'm always open to fresh material, and years of experience have taught me that funny stuff happens every day in our lives. I'm never surprised when a real life conversation winds up in one of my gigs. Like the day Anita and I were enjoying Leah's condo pool the past summer.

Several other elderly residents of the "pool pals" had joined us and were *shmoozing* about various topics when the conversation turned to the "noodles" they were using in the pool. Noodles were long, slender, foam tubes the old folks slipped under their arms to help them swim, float or just maintain their balance. Almost everyone used a noodle.

"Men have an advantage with these things," said a red-haired woman who was married and divorced three times. She liked telling shady stories.

"Why is that?" asked a bald man in his 70s.

"It gives them a fourth leg."

"They need it," said another woman. "Sometimes their third leg doesn't work very well."

The thrice-married woman said dryly, "It never did."

The other women in the circle, divorced or widowed, whooped and hollered.

The story had just enough raunchiness to tickle my aging audience at my next show, especially the women.

The outdoor pool was a popular place to hang out in the summer. Actually, it was open from Memorial Day until after Labor Day, sometimes late in September, weather permitting. On an average day as many as 20 or more people would gather, occupying tables with umbrellas, folding chairs and lounge chairs. Some of them would form small groups and *shmooze* for hours. Others avoided the sun by filling chairs positioned under trees. They read or napped or talked with others nearby. Groups of women, grasping their noodles, would slip into the pool, form a small circle, and converse. Occasionally, a man would join them. He was welcomed because women outnumbered men around five to one.

The group came from all over the country, several from the East Coast, two from California, one each from Texas, Illinois and Florida. They brought their regional accents with them—from a Bostoner's insistence on inserting an unnecessary *r* as President Kennedy did with *Cuber* and a man from east Texas whose speech was almost unintelligible. They sat close enough so they could talk to each other without shouting. They wore age-appropriate bathing suits, so there were no bikinis among the women, except for one. She was the youngest of the ladies, short and a little on the plump side. Dark brown hair flowed below her shoulders. Her charms were noticed by one of the few men in the group. He was tall and thin as a one-iron. Soon they were considered a couple. They sat close together where she often stroked his back. If there was any jealousy, it was pretty much hidden, except for one woman who glared at the couple constantly.

The others ranged in age from about sixty to eighty-five. The old fart was me. Some of the others were remarkably fit for their ages, serious devotees of the fitness center on the grounds. Two women were divorcees who referred to their ex-husbands as "the jerk" or some other uncomplimentary term. One of the men was a recent widower who was still grieving. The group worked hard to help him through his sorrow. Although they seemed to like each other there was one discordant note.

Among the few men, most of them unmarried, there was one guy who had a reputation for being a womanizer. That is, he dated quite a few of them at different times. Probably slept with some of them—if not all—at least that was the prevailing assumption. Then he'd get bored and start sniffing around. I had the feeling that most of the women knew exactly what he was up to, but some would allow him into their beds anyway. Lust doesn't go away just because you're over sixty.

They were mostly of similar political persuasion. This being an election year, they often talked politics. At other times they shared stories about shopping, their families, or television shows they liked. Other than the occasional tale of romantic escapades, I rarely heard anything that could be considered gossip. They teased each other in fun. Food trucks parked nearby, and they shared snacks and drinks.

When the pool closed at summer's end, it was a sad occasion. However, the HOA left the chairs and tables available for a few more weeks until they were finally removed for winter storage. Some of the members departed Colorado for Arizona, California or Mexico where they had winter getaways. The remaining members of Leah's group attended weekly pot-luck suppers at their apartments to continue gathering, including Christmas week. When a fun-loving woman learned that one of the men was turning ninety during Christmas week, she decided to put on a show. Wearing a Marilyn Monroe wig and slinky black dress, she approached the oldtimer and breathlessly sang "Happy Birthday, Mr. Horowitz." The others roared with laughter.

I put together enough gags from my notebook to complete my routine for next Saturday night, and then turned my attention to the deaths at Mervin

Gardens. Actually, I got online and searched the internet for general information about deaths in Denver County the past year. What I found was not particularly surprising.

In the previous year there were 4,657 total deaths in the county. The Medical Examiner's office said 3,299 deaths were attributed to "natural causes." Almost three out of four. So it raised the question: what constitutes "a natural death?" Most people use that expression when referring to older people. They say things like "he died of old age"—which really doesn't mean anything. So what exactly what does "natural causes" mean?

The Centers for Disease Control and Prevention (CDC) said there were forty-six categories of natural causes of death. The top five were heart disease, cancer, chronic lower respiratory disease, stroke and Alzheimer's disease. Among the cancer deaths, the most common were lung, colon/rectum/anus, and breast, pancreatic and prostate. But Leah insisted Sidney's death and the others were actually murders disguised as "natural," but were in reality deaths due to "non-natural" causes. Of these, the most common were poisoning, motor vehicle accidents, falls and suicide. In Denver County, homicides accounted for nine percent of the deaths. But no guns were associated with the deaths in Leah's building.

I looked again at the list of most common causes of unnatural deaths. At the top was "accidental poisoning." But what if it wasn't accidental? I made a note to look into that later, and then started listing the deaths by name, some personal information and the date of their deaths. I printed the list and looked at the details I had compiled chronologically. All were in the current year, compared to only one death the previous year.

- January 13. Rita Altman, 78. Cause of death: respiratory failure. A widow. She lived in the same building as Leah for the past four years.

- February 2. Russell Barringer, 82. Heart attack. Widower, retired psychiatrist and resident for six years.

- March 17. Janet Christie, 89. Liver and spleen failure. She had lived there 13 years.

-April 25. Arlene Morgan, 65. Drowning. Her body was found in the indoor pool. She'd been a resident for almost four years.

-May 1, the most recent. Leah's gentleman friend Sidney Luft, 73. Respiratory failure. It was the fifth death.

I scanned the list and then studied it carefully, attempting to memorize the basic facts. I wanted to be able to recall them without referring to the printed copy. I turned the sheet of paper face down and recited the names, ages, and causes of death, stumbling a bit on how long they'd lived at Mervin Gardens, but overall I was satisfied that I could remember the basics. The activity made me a little tired, so I headed for my bedroom to take a short nap. An incoming telephone call intercepted me.

These days I seldom answered my phone, waiting to see if the caller would leave a message. But something made me pick up the receiver.

"Hello," I said.

"Mr. Brand?"

"Yes."

"Mr. Izzy Brand, the comic performer at the comedy club?"

I've been careful about keeping my landline number fairly private so I don't usually get calls from people I don't know. This was a woman's voice, probably an older woman, but with an assertive tone.

"Yes, that is me," I said a bit anxiously. "Who is this?"

"My name is not important. I'm calling to tell you not to believe what Leah Lamont is telling you—that the recent deaths at Mervin Gardens were murders. That's nonsense. That Lamont woman is crazy. She still thinks she's doing drama in the movies, or whatever. Don't waste your time on her fantasies."

"Are you a neighbor? Do you live in her build....?"

I never got an answer to my questions because the caller hung up before I completed asking them. I replaced the receiver, wondering who this woman was and how she knew that Leah had asked me to investigate. Obviously she knew Leah and she knew about the deaths. I looked at my caller ID. It said the caller's number was unknown. I opened my little notebook and made an entry.

Because I've always been obstinate enough to pursue something people advise against, I now felt compelled to launch a serious investigation. First order of business? Learn more about all the deceased and a helluva lot more about their neighbors. I called Leah and told her I was coming over to pick up her list of fellow occupants in her building.

Then, before I could leave my apartment, my telephone rang again. This time, the surprise was almost as great. It was my niece, my sister's only child.

"Hi, Uncle Izzy, it's Rebecca."

"Hello, sweetheart, I'm tickled to hear from you. How are you?"

I sensed a hesitation. "I'm in Denver. Can I come over and see you?"

"Of course. I have to run an errand but I'll be back in an hour."

"I'll see you at six. Will that be okay?"

"Excellent, honey. We'll have dinner."

"See you then. Bye."

I replaced the receiver feeling a bit apprehensive. I hadn't talked to my niece since her tenth wedding anniversary about six months ago. I had called to congratulate her. She sounded happy at the time, but now she seemed preoccupied, maybe even troubled. Then Anita called.

"Are you coming for dinner?"

"Not tonight, hon. My niece is in town. How about tomorrow?"

"Okay, see you then."

"When do you want me?"

"About six."

"You missed an opportunity to make a joke. You could have said: 'All the time, Big Guy.'"

"You're not a big guy. You never were."

"Young fella?"

"You're no spring chicken."

"It's getting harder to make you laugh."

"It's getting harder for you to get hard."

"Are you complaining?"

"No, my dear, not at all. It's to be expected at your age."

Oh, boy, everybody thinks they're a comedian. Wait. She was joking, wasn't she?

SIX

LEAH HAD DONE HER homework. She greeted me with a sheaf of papers containing not only the names and apartment numbers of every occupant in her building, but also some tidbits about them, including whether they were owners or renters and were living alone or with spouses or companions. She told me the HOA had a policy of limiting renters to 20 percent of the units, but she thought there were fewer than that. Most of the units were owner-occupied, all of them by people who were financially well-off. A majority were widows who were left considerable estates. Even the divorcees enjoyed significant settlements for life. She invited me to stay for dinner but I told her I was meeting with my niece later. While there, I asked her why she was so convinced that the deaths in her building were all homicides.

"I knew these people, Izzy. While some of them may have been a bit feeble or struggling with an illness, they were still active and alert. I'd see them at various activities we have here. Some played bridge or attended discussion groups. Others played golf or tennis or swam regularly in the pool. You wouldn't expect them to up and die suddenly."

"The grim reaper doesn't send a text message," I said. "He just shows up, especially in a place like this that's full of elderly people. When their time is up, it's up."

Leah fashioned an expression of dogged exasperation. "I know that, Izzy. Nevertheless, how do you explain that no other building in the complex has had so many deaths in such a short period of time? And there are five individual buildings here. Only in my building do people seem to die so often. Five in five months! Why is that?"

"Five buildings, five deaths, five months," I said. "Maybe there's a killer with a fetish for numbers—or maybe it's just a coincidence," I added hastily, aware that I sounded a bit lame.

"I don't believe in coincidences," she shot back. "Things happen for a reason."

She spoke with the conviction of a true believer, like someone who knows they are absolutely right no matter what counter arguments are offered. When I left her apartment, an image remained in my mind. It was of Leah, standing in her living room, her feet spread slightly apart, hands on hips, a determined look on her face.

I took the elevator to the lobby where a woman in a wheelchair intercepted me before I left the building.

"Hello, Mr. Brand," she greeted me with a smile.

"Hello. Do I know you?"

"We've never been introduced, but I've seen you around here with Mrs. Lamont's friend. I forgot her name. Ann something, I think."

"Anita. Her name is Anita. And what is yours?"

"I am Margrette Tripp. I live on the same floor as Mrs. Lamont. She's been quite upset recently over the deaths in our building and now, especially, the sudden passing of her gentleman friend. I should stop by and offer my condolences, but I want to give her a little more time."

I wondered how she knew about Sidney's death since it was too soon for a death notice to appear in the newspaper. "How do you know he passed away?"

"Probably from someone in the building. News like that gets around."

I studied her for a moment. A small woman. A pinched face. No lipstick. Despite being confined to a wheelchair, she possessed enough self-awareness to color her hair to hide its march toward grayness. Black slacks, a gray blouse and low-heeled shoes signaled a no-nonsense attitude.

"Nice meeting you, Miss Tripp," I said

"It's Mrs. Tripp. I lost my husband six years ago."

"I'm sorry. Enjoy your day."

I left the lobby and got into my car, thinking about my niece. She never before had come to Colorado just to see me. She said she wanted to talk to me about something, and that she had come alone. Obviously, something was bothering her and wanted to share it with me. I headed for my apartment in the Golden Triangle neighborhood feeling a little anxious about our meeting.

***

The way George greeted me you'd think I'd left

him alone for a week. He was all over me with moist kisses and wagging stump of a tail, what little there was of it. Then he raced to the hall, snatched up his leash on the floor and raced back to me with an expression that clearly said, "Let's go. You should be ashamed of yourself for neglecting me. I've waited long enough!" After four years in my apartment, he's still trying to convince me he's the Alpha dog here.

I took him downstairs, greeted Walter, our doorman, and followed George outdoors to his favorite tree down the block. I guess he really had to go because he relieved himself immediately. But instead of turning back to our building he decided to explore the area. No surprise there. Still on the leash, he pulled me down the block to a vacant sidewalk bench where homeless people sometimes sat. He checked it out, and then examined a nearby shrub. The sun was setting and I knew Rebecca would be arriving shortly. "C'mon, George. We gotta go." I tugged the leash gently and guided him home.

Rebecca was waiting for me in the lobby. She threw her arms around me and kissed me on the cheek. "Good to see you, Uncle Izzy." She's called me that since she learned to talk, only it used to be Uncle Itty.

I gave her strong hug. "And I love seeing you, sweetheart. Do you want to go upstairs or do you just want to have dinner somewhere?"

"I'm not very hungry. Can we just talk in your place for a while?"

Obviously she wanted to get down to business. "Sure. I can fix us something in a hurry if you'd like."

I was glad my cleaning lady had come by the day before because my place was decent. I know how many women size up people by the way they keep their homes. Claudia comes every two weeks and does a good job cleaning the two bathrooms, living room and kitchen. She vacuums, dusts and does a little polishing. My office presents a challenge because it's cluttered with stacks of paper. I know where everything is so I don't want her moving things. She just dusts around the stacks, does the window blinds and the fan blades.

Rebecca parked herself in my wing-back arm chair. At the age of forty-two, she was still a strikingly good-looking woman. Almond-shaped brown eyes, high cheek bones and shapely lips. She had chestnut-colored hair that fell below her shoulders. Her fit body advertised her rigorous exercise program. She and her husband never had children so she had the time to take care of herself despite the demands of her advertising job on Madison Avenue in Manhattan.

"How is Malcolm?" I asked.

She pulled a cigarette from her purse and lit up without asking permission. Although I'm not a smoker—I gave it up in my thirties—I did not protest.

"He's okay health-wise, I guess, if that's what you mean. I haven't seen him in two weeks. I've been staying with a friend."

"Is there a problem, honey?"

"There's been a problem for a long time. Too long. That's why I'm here. When I was a little girl, and later as a teenager, I knew I could always go to you for a heart-to-heart talk. You never judged me, Uncle Izzy, you just listened. You didn't offer advice unless I asked for it."

"Are you going to ask for advice tonight?"

"Maybe."

"So, what's the problem? Is Malcolm cheating on you?"

"No, it's nothing like that. It's more subtle. In a way, it's more hurtful."

"What could be more hurtful than a cheating husband?"

She pulled the half-smoked cigarette from her lips and looked for an ashtray. "I'm sorry, Uncle Izzy. I forgot you don't smoke anymore."

"That's okay, honey." I opened the drawer of a nearby table where I kept an ashtray for such occasions and handed it to her.

She crushed the butt. "What's more hurtful is an uncommunicative husband," she said. "A husband who doesn't talk, who just shuts down like he's suddenly lost his voice. He eats dinner in silence and then parks himself in front of the TV until late at night, and then goes to bed without saying a word. That kind of husband."

I wasn't sure how to reply, except to say a feeble: "Wow, that's tough." I needed time to process what she'd just told me. I knew they had no financial problems. They lived in an upscale condo on

Manhattan's west side and owned a getaway in Boca Raton. What would make him isolate himself like that? I had no idea. "Is he angry at you for something and doesn't want to talk about it?" I asked.

"No. We usually agreed on everything—except conversation. Most couples like us talked about what our day was like. They found something to talk about. He didn't. He just crawled down within himself. I felt like I was living alone. It was driving me crazy. Then he disappeared."

"What do you mean?"

"He packed a bag and left. Never said a word. I don't know where he is and I haven't heard from him. I called his boss and learned he's okay, but his boss wouldn't tell me anything else. Said it's between me and Malcolm to resolve. I'm so frustrated."

"You've been married 10 years. How long has this been going on?"

She opened her purse and extracted another cigarette, lit it, and blew a cloud into the air. I really wanted to ask her not to smoke, but I realized she was doing it to calm herself and I didn't want to add to her agitation. Besides, I could freshen the room after she left. She looked at the butt between her fingers as if she didn't realize it was there. "Damn! I'm sorry, Uncle Izzy. I lit up again without even thinking. I'm such a pill." Then she remembered my question.

"It's been about five months since he decided to become a sphinx. We were probably a normal couple until then. We did lots of things together—golf, tennis, bowling, joining friends for dinner out. We shared our work experiences. He always had interesting stories to tell about Wall Street, things you never read about in the paper or saw on TV. I thought we had a good marriage. Then he changed."

"Without a reason?"

"He just stopped talking. At first I thought he had something on his mind he didn't want to talk about. I asked him if he had a problem that he needed to tell me. He just shook his head."

"That certainly sounds strange," I said. "Have you thought about going for therapy? A marriage counselor?"

"I suggested it. He wasn't interested. He said it

was unnecessary, but I was going out of my mind. Now I'm thinking about a divorce, or at least a separation. That's why I'm here, Uncle Izzy. What do you think? "

There it was. She wanted my opinion! Maybe advice! I didn't know what to say. I said the only thing that came to mind. "Have you talked to your mom?"

"No. She's always thought the world of Malcolm. I'm afraid she'll blame me, that it's something I've said or done. I couldn't handle that."

"But she's your mother. Shouldn't she know?"

"Not yet. Please don't tell her, Uncle Izzy."

Wow! This is a tough one. I remembered times when she was much younger and she'd come to me with problems she considered earth-shattering, like the cliques she confronted in middle-school and the boys she met in high school. The only serious problem occurred when an assistant professor hit on her when she was a senior at Tufts. I knew a dean there and was able to put a leash on the bastard, at least on the campus. She weathered that storm and went on to graduate with honors. *What can I tell her now?*

"Honey, let me think about this. Can I get back to you in a few days?"

"Of course, Uncle Izzy. I know I blind-sided you."

"Okay, let's get something to eat. Do you still like Mexican dishes? There's a new place I town that'll set your hair on fire."

She grinned. "Sounds wonderful. I'm game."

***

I woke the next morning feeling uneasy. Suddenly my plate seemed full. I had promised Anita and Leah that I would investigate the deaths at Mervin Gardens, and now my niece had laid a serious problem on my doorstep. In addition, I had to prepare for my gig on Saturday night. I had a general idea of what I wanted to do, but some careful tweaking was in order. Timely gags were always popular so I had to be aware of current happenings. Then my thoughts went back to Rebecca and I recalled the long spell when her mother and I were estranged. Anita played a major role in our reconciliation.

I had told Anita that my sister and I hadn't talked for a long time. Coincidentally, Anita had met Edith at some kind of conference and they became friends. Anita encouraged me to make an effort to reconnect and suggested I write a short letter. "She's your only living relative," she told me, "besides your niece. You should be closer."

I sent off a note and was surprised to receive a warm response. We've been in touch fairly regularly since then. While we were estranged I somehow grew even closer to Rebecca. We spoke frequently as she was growing up, perhaps because there were no male adults in her life after her father died of cancer at an early age and her mother never remarried. To her credit, Edith never interfered in my relationship with her daughter.

So now after 10 years of marriage, Rebecca was contemplating divorce or a separation and wanted my views. Right now I had no idea what to tell her. As a widower for almost fifty years I had no personal experience that might be helpful. When confronted with problems for which I didn't have a ready answer, I looked for help. Since meeting Anita, I always turned to her.

When I called her later that night, she asked: "How was your dinner with Rebecca?"

"Dinner was just fine. But she asked for my opinion about a problem she's having and I frankly don't know what to tell her. I need to tell you about it. Can you meet me for lunch tomorrow?"

She suggested a Chinese place in Cherry Creek near her office. I made a note and then began preparing for my Saturday night gig. I also decided I'd begin to look into the deaths at Mervin Gardens. But where to start? Obviously, I needed to learn more about the victims. Carlos was satisfied the deaths were natural so I had a clear path.

SEVEN

LIVING IN CHERRY CREEK North, Anita always surprised me with her first-hand knowledge of delightful and convenient dining places. The Chinese restaurant she suggested was on a commercial block of quirky shops featuring unique items. The restaurant sat just below street level, requiring patrons to negotiate a few steps down. I found Anita sitting near a window that offered an ankle view of pedestrians strolling by. A great place to sit for anyone with an appreciation of shapely female legs.

"So what did you learn from Rebecca?" she asked, getting right down to business.

I told her about our conversation, her leaving her husband and living with a friend and the reason why. "She's contemplating a divorce or at least a legal separation. She wanted my opinion. Frankly, I don't know what to tell her. I was hoping you might have some ideas."

"That's a sticky one to lay on an uncle. Obviously, she must have enormous trust in you, Izzy. She's chosen you to be her confidante and advisor."

"Yeah, well to paraphrase Tevye in *Fiddler* when he's talking to God, "I wish she would choose someone else for a change."

"In her heart, you are her Tevye—the font of all wisdom, the solver of problems."

"I'm honored, but I'm humbled because I have no wisdom to share with her. I can't solve her problem."

The server appeared and we gave her our orders—a small salad for Anita and a plate of Egg Foo Young with vegetables for me. When the young lady left, Anita continued our conversation.

"Obviously, something is bothering her husband. It could be any number of things. Perhaps he got a diagnosis about an illness he doesn't want to share with his wife. Maybe he lost his job or is in danger of losing it. Has he taken a serious hit in the stock market? Would she be aware if their financial situation were perilous?"

"She's pretty savvy about financial things. I doubt that could be a cause."

"She's savvy about a lot of things. I wonder if he could be jealous of her—her achievements compared to his? Does he see her as an over-achiever? Does she earn more money? Maybe he has a notion that she's been cheating on *him!* There are so many things. She really needs to get him to open up."

"She's tried that but he refused. That's why she's so frustrated."

"Has he attempted to contact her since he left?"

"Apparently not. She said she hasn't heard from him."

"He may be too proud. Men can be like that."

"Possessing no such flaw, I know not whereof you speak, dear madam."

Anita flashed me a skeptical smile. "Of course not, your lordship."

We finished our meals and prepared to leave. She asked: "Were they making love before he left"

"She didn't say and I didn't have the *chutzpah* to ask her."

"When did *that* ever stop you?"

I paid the check and said, "Thanks for your input, honey. It's helpful."

"Best of luck," she said, kissing me before we headed for our cars.

***

I went home determined to find an explanation for Malcolm's behavior. Then I had an idea to put a tail on Malcolm. I'd find out where he goes, who does he meet, and then maybe learn why he acts the way he does at home. I knew he worked as an upper level manager for a corporation in Manhattan and that's where he'd spend his work hours. At least, that's where he should be.

And I knew someone who, I hoped, would be able to answer those questions.

Mike Halloran was a classmate at North High School when we were growing up on Denver's West Side in the '40s. Wanting to experience the Big City, he applied to Columbia in Manhattan and was accepted, but dropped out after completing his junior year. He was immediately drafted into the Army. After two years at Fort Monmouth in New Jersey, half that time serving as a military policeman corralling boisterous soldiers in Jersey Shore towns from Asbury Park to Cape May, he was discharged. He returned to New York City to find his path in life. To no one's surprise, he became a private investigator.

Mike and I were not the closest of friends, but close enough so that we stayed in touch over the years. He invited me to his wedding and dropped in at the club several times to catch my show whenever he was in town. His business grew and the last time we talked he told me he had a half-dozen PIs working for him, most of them retired detectives.

I found his telephone number in my contact list and called him. A receptionist told me he was out of the office. Did I want to leave a message?

"Just tell him I have a job for him."

Then I turned my attention to my upcoming Saturday night gig. Poring over my gag file, I found one I hadn't used all year.

Henry's mother-in-law confronted him one Christmas and said, "You haven't given me a present in years."

"Yes, I remember," Henry said, "it was a cemetery plot. But you never used it."

I decided to use that one and several others, and made some notes on where in my routine

I would place the gags. Then I practiced my routine with an eye on the clock to make sure I had enough material to cover my forty-minute slot. It was okay if I went a bit over the scheduled time—my audiences don't walk out until my show is complete. At least they haven't before. But you never know what the next audience will do.

After a twenty-minute nap, I sat down in my recliner and reviewed the notes Leah had given me about her expired neighbors. I was looking for anything they had in common. The victims ranged in age from 65 to 89. They all had lived alone in Leah's building. Some of them kept pets.

Other than Leah's brief notes, there was not much to go on, certainly not enough to develop a pattern of behavior about these people. I would have to contact their next next-of-kin and neighbors to learn more, but I thought I'd start first with the association's business manager.

A telephone call would have been the most convenient approach but, in my experience, face-face-communications almost always brings better results. I drove to Mervin Gardens and went to the administrative offices, looking for the business manager, and introduced myself.

Her name was Angelica Cerrone, she'd been on the job for six years, and she wasn't too happy to talk to me. "I'm really quite busy, Mr. Brand. What do you want to know?"

"You've had an extraordinary number of deaths this year in Building 2," I said. I gave her a slip of paper with the names of the former residents. She took a quick glance and returned the slip of paper. "I know who they were."

"What about your other buildings? Do you have a record of the deaths that occurred there, too?"

"That's a strange question. Why would we keep such a record? People die all the time, especially in a complex of elderly residents. And what business is that of yours?"

Oh, boy, I thought, this is going to be a tough interview. "I've been asked to look into the deaths by a friend who is one of your home owners. And I agree that death is common in communities like this. I'm just trying to determine if the number of deaths in Building 2 is an anomaly. Is it normal, or more than usual?"

"Well, I'm afraid I can't answer that. We don't

keep those kind of records. Was there something else you wanted to know?"

"Of the folks who died in Building Two, do you know how they spent their time? I assume they weren't working so they had idle time."

"You'd be surprised how busy these old-timers can be." A glint of recognition suddenly flashed in her eyes. "Oh, I know you. You're Mrs. Lamont's friend, the comedian."

"That's me."

"My mother is a fan."

"I'm glad to hear it. Here, let me leave a couple of tickets for her for my next show."

"Thank you," she said, picking up the tickets and putting them in her purse. "She'll be delighted to get these, Mr. Brand. Now, what was it you asked me?"

"I was wondering how those people spent their idle time."

"As I recall, Mrs. Morgan and Mrs. Altman were pretty active. They belonged to several clubs here at Mervin Gardens, and both had a circle of friends. Dr. Barringer and Mrs. Christie were less so. And, of course, Leah Lamont's friend, Mr.

Luft, was active in various clubs. He especially liked playing tennis and using our pool."

"Were any of them close friends?"

"I really don't know about that. Being neighbors, they surely knew each other, but I don't know if they socialized, except for the scheduled social gatherings we have here, like a dinner during the Christmas holiday season. And, of course, some residents host an occasional get-together for their neighbors."

"Do you have the names of the hosts?"

She hesitated. "Not really, but telling you that might be an invasion of their privacy," she blurted.

"That would be true if they were alive, Miss Cerrone, but they're not," I said.

"Nevertheless, I don't think I should get into that." She was getting tight-lipped. Before she shut down on me completely, I needed to get her list of emergency contacts—the names of the next of kin that all the residents left in their files she kept in her office. Leah told me that was standard practice. I asked for those names and placed two more show tickets on her desk. "Maybe you and your husband might like to go, too," I said.

She glanced at the tickets and then went to a file cabinet. A few moments later, she brought five file folders to her desk and began going through them. "Do you want to jot these down?"

I pulled my little pad from my pocket and clicked my ballpoint pen. "Ready when you are," I said.

She began reciting names. "Mrs. Donna Paltz, daughter of Rita Altman. Phoenix, Arizona. Do you want phone numbers?"

"Yes, indeed."

She gave me the Paltz number and went on. "Dr. Andrew Barringer, son of Dr. Russell Barringer, Denver."

"Father and son were doctors?"

"The father was a retired psychiatrist. His son specializes in respiratory medicine here in Denver. At St. Joseph Hospital."

She continued until she had given me the names of five family members, the cities where they lived, and their phone numbers. I thanked her and then decided to gamble that I might get some more information from her.

"Did any of them come to you with a problem,

something out of the ordinary?"

She glared at me and said, "I really have to get back to work. Goodbye Mr. Brand."

Oh, well, I've always been a lousy gambler. I almost regretted giving her the tickets. That wasn't much, I thought, but it was a start. At least I had a list of contacts from whom, I hoped, I could obtain more information about the victims. Where else to go while I'm here? Most adult community complexes have some kind of security staff, I knew, and Mervin Gardens was no exception. I left Miss Personality and headed for the office of the complex's security department, called Security Patrol. Their chief was attending a meeting somewhere and I wound up speaking with a young female officer.

Miranda Martinez greeted me with curious brown eyes and a skeptical expression. Big-bosomed, her breasts seemed ready to burst out of her buttoned, tight-fitting black shirt. Ditto her buttocks from her equally snug black trousers. A black Glock sat in a holster on her waist. Focusing on her face to avoid further distraction, I introduced myself.

"What can I do for you, Mr. Brand?" she asked in a cadence that blended police professionalism with a cultural caution.

I explained my mission.

"So you're an amateur sleuth?" she said with a slightly condescending tone.

"I suppose you can say that. I've been pretty successful." I asked her how long she'd been on the job.

"Going on four years. They hired me on right out of the Army. I served in Iraq before my discharge. Of course, I needed some training. Keeping an eye on elderly people is not the same as fighting Arabs."

I felt encouraged by her reply. At least that meant that she had a history working at Mervin Gardens and would likely know all or most of the deceased.

"I was wondering, Officer Martinez, if you ever encountered these people—the ones who died this year, apparently of natural causes?"

"Refresh my memory. Do you have a list of their names?"

I handed her the slip of paper and watched her

study the list for a moment. "Rita Altman was always locking herself out of her apartment. She kept a vase on a small table outside her apartment and I finally persuaded her to put a spare key in the vase. That seemed to help. Didn't hear from her for quite a while."

I scribbled a note in my pad. "Anybody else?"

"We got a call from Dr. Barringer's son one day. He said he couldn't reach his father. We entered his apartment and found him unconscious on the floor in his bedroom. We helped him regain consciousness and then took him to the ER for an examination. Eventually they discharged him. We never learned why he passed out."

I made another note and waited.

"And of course there was Arlene Morgan, the lady who was found drowned in our pool last month. She was a regular at the pool and an accomplished swimmer. Still don't know how that happened."

"Was anyone with her?"

"No. It was late at night, about 10:30. We keep the pool open till 11, and she was alone."

"Who found her?"

The Mervin Gardens Murders

"I did. I was making my rounds. I pulled her out of the water and tried to resuscitate her but she was gone. I called the police. The coroner ruled it an accidental drowning."

"Was there anything out of place around the pool, anything that caught your attention?"

"Well, the chairs were sort of scrambled."

"What do you mean?"

"The pool staff stacks the chairs about 9 p.m. after most of the swimmers have left. Some of those chairs were scattered around the pool when I found her. The police asked me about them, too."

"I've seen security cameras around the pool," I said. "Were they checked?"

The question seemed to catch her off guard. "Yes, but I don't think they've been reviewed."

"You might want to take a look," I suggested.

I made another note.

"In your contacts with these people over the years, was there anything else out of the ordinary or suspicious about them or their activities or conversations with you?"

"Well, like I said, we never could explain why

Dr. Barringer passed out in his bedroom or why a skilled swimmer like Mrs. Morgan drowned. In the end it made no difference. They all died natural deaths, although Mrs. Morgan's drowning was accidental."

"Leah Lamont doesn't think so."

"Yeah, I heard that. But the police never investigated. They're satisfied with the medical examiner's reports. So why are *you* snooping around? *There was that condescending tone again.* I reminded myself that Officer Martinez had never graduated a police academy and was hardly in a position to criticize my sleuthing.

Her demeanor was beginning to get on my nerves. Before replying with a bit of sarcasm, my usual response under the circumstances, I decided to end our conversation. "Thanks for your time, Officer, and for the information."

"You're welcome. By the way, you really should leave police work to the professionals."

She had to have the last word. That's okay, I thought. I've heard the same comment from others, including my friend Detective Collins and even my late wife, Clara, who sometimes comes to me at night and asks me why an old man like me has become a homicide detective. *Are you meshuga, Izzy?* she asks me.

It's not like I'm actually *looking* for murders to solve. Is it my fault they keep coming my way? Besides, who says these deaths at Mervin Gardens were actually murders? So far it's only Leah Lamont who thinks so. Then why am I knocking myself out? Because Anita, the dearest lady in my life, asked me to look into it. I've never been able to say *no* to that woman.

EIGHT

UPON RETURNING TO MY forest green Mustang in the Mervin Gardens parking lot, I found a slip of paper on my front seat. It read: *Stop nosing around. It could be detrimental to your health.*

Since it was a sunny day in early May and getting warm, I had left my front windows open about two inches to keep the heat from building up. Someone took the opportunity to drop the typewritten note through the opening. I scanned the note again. The note was folded twice. I pondered the writer's intention. Was this some kind of sick joke? Or was it serious?

If these deaths were all of natural causes, why would anybody threaten me? Then I thought: *If I needed any reason to pursue the investigation, I certainly had one now.*

Suddenly, this was no longer simply a favor I was doing for Anita and her friend, Leah. Apparently someone was concerned enough to fear my intervention. Who would feel that way other than a person with something to hide—like a killer?

I folded the note and put it in my pocket, almost fully convinced that Leah's instincts were correct. Only a few hours earlier I thought of Leah's suspicions as those of an overly imaginative elderly woman. Now I viewed her concern in a new light and I needed to tell Anita. And also my detective friend, Carlos. I drove to Anita's place in Cherry Creek North. Since it was almost 5 o'clock, I knew her home office hours were over and she would be available to talk.

Her reaction was predictable. She was immediately alarmed. "This validates Leah's suspicions, Izzy. You're being warned. You need to tell Carlos right away."

I said, "I've investigated murders before, sweetheart, and solved them without suffering even a slight cut or bruise." Well, that wasn't entirely true. I did get tapped over the head once, but I survived.

"This is different, Izzy. Someone clearly thinks you are capable of discovering his secrets. That person wants you to stop immediately. Please let Carlos know."

There was something in her voice that I had not

heard before. She spoke with a slight tremor that gave evidence of her concern for my well-being. I was moved enough to put my arms around her and kiss her. "Nothing will happen to me, sweetheart. You know that I'm indestructible."

What I intended to be humorous had a curious effect. She began to cry and then placed her hands on my face. "Izzy, you don't know who you're dealing with here. It could be a deranged person, but a very clever one. He has figured out how to disguise a series of murders, and make these deaths look natural. Even the medical examiner has been fooled. That's why there's never been a police investigation. I don't want anything to happen to you."

She continued to sob, her face pressed against mine. I could feel her tears on my cheeks. Suddenly I had a kind of epiphany. While we had known each other for years, and I had told her many times that I loved her, even proposed, she had never expressed her love for me. But now, fearing I was in danger, she was showing me how she felt. My heart filled with joy. We held each tightly as she continued to cry while I tried to console her.

Finally, I said, "Okay, honey, I'll go to Police Headquarters and see Carlos."

"Turn it over to him," she responded with relief in her voice. "Let him find the killer."

"Is it all right if I advise him?"

She was still in my arms but she pushed me away. "No. I want you to stay away from this case. Completely. Promise me, Izzy."

I thought she was going to cry again so I quickly promised her. I headed for her door and my visit to Police Headquarters.

***

Denver's Major Crimes Division, which includes the Homicide/Robbery unit, is housed in a 70-year-old red-brick building of three stories on Cherokee Street in the heart of downtown. A large parking lot enclosed by a chain-link fence sits forlornly adjacent to the building. The desk sergeant recognized me.

"Hey, Izzy, you here to see Carlos?"

"Yeah, I hope he's in."

"Think so. I'll ring his phone." After a moment he said: "He's on the way down."

Detective Carlos Collins greeted me with

a typical Irish grin set against his Hispanic complexion. He had married a vivacious lass named Erin Aragon who, like Carlos, was half Hispanic, half Irish. She was now eight months pregnant.

I recalled Carlos' father, a cop killed by an armed burglar when Carlos was fourteen. Against his mother's wishes, Carlos joined the Denver PD after graduation from the University of Colorado. I watched him rise in the ranks until he became a detective three years ago. His promotion, he told me, honored his father's memory.

He embraced me in a bear hug and then released me with a frown on his face. "It's always good to see you, Izzy, but something tells me this is more than a social call. Is it about those deaths at Mervin Gardens?"

I started to tell him about the note I found in my car, but he interrupted me and said, "Let's go upstairs."

I followed him to his desk, one of about a dozen on the second floor. He motioned me to a straight-back chair and lowered himself into a more comfortable–looking desk chair with arms and wheels.

"Do you have the note?"

I pulled it from my pocket and handed it to him. He grasped a corner of the paper and placed the note on his desk. "No sense in mucking it up. Maybe we can lift some prints from it." He read the message quickly and said: "Sounds like you've pissed off someone, Izzy. And he's very unhappy."

"Anita is frightened. I've never seen her react like this before. She insisted I bring it right to you. She wants me to drop the whole thing."

"Well, of course she's absolutely right. I've been telling you the same thing for years, but you're a stubborn old man. You like being a dick."

I flashed him a faux expression of pain. "I trust you mean my success in solving homicides."

"Oh, yeah, that too," he grinned. Then, he turned serious and said: "This note makes it police business, Izzy, so it's time for you to bow out and leave it to me."

"But the medical examiner said the deaths were all natural," I said. "Are you opening an investigation?"

"Not officially. This note could be a harmless prank. But I should follow up on it."

"It's all yours," I assured him. "Just let me know what you may need from me."

A picture of dogged exasperation appeared on his face. He rose from his chair and patted me on the cheek. "You want me to tell Anita that you're not keeping your promise to her?"

"No, but I know you're busy with other cases. I just wanted you to know I'm available to help if you need it."

"Thanks for the offer. I'm investigating a scam of an old-timer who lost twenty grand of his life's savings, but I should be wrapping that up pretty soon."

"Sounds interesting. I'd like to know more about it sometime. Maybe I can work it into my gig. Most of my audience consists of old-timers, you know. It could be a kind of public service announcement— if I could find some humor in it."

"Oh, you will. You can find a joke in almost anything."

"Yeah, well, so far I haven't found anything to laugh about with the murders at Mervin Gardens."

There, I'd said it. In my mind I now agreed with Leah. These deaths were not natural. They were homicides. And like it or not, I was already in the middle of it.

As if to confirm my feelings, I found another note when I returned to my car. It read:

You took my note to your detective friend. Very bad decision. Now I am really mad. Your fate is sealed, Mr. Brand—and that's no joke!

NINE

I CAN'T SAY THE note stunned me but it did shake me up a bit. In none of my previous homicide cases did I feel the killer was stalking me. Never before had I been threatened. This case was different. It had become personal, exactly what Anita feared. The first note scared her terribly. If I told her about the second note it would only add to her fear. But how could I keep it from her? Ironically, she was the one who implored me to investigate. I agreed to snoop around only as a favor—to her and her friend, Leah. I didn't believe these deaths were homicides. But now I did.

The killer made a mistake when he started writing notes to me. He made it personal and by doing so he convinced me that Leah's suspicions were correct. Now I was determined to nail the son-of-a-bitch. I promised Anita I would let the Denver PD handle it, but this second note triggered a spark in me. Before you tell Carlos, I lectured myself, at least talk to some of the victims' next-of-kin. Maybe I'll get lucky and learn why these people were targeted. And then, maybe, I'll get even luckier and learn who the killer was.

If things start to go south, I can always call in the cavalry. I can always call Carlos.

***

Seated behind the wheel of my car, I pulled my notepad from my pocket, flipped to the pages that contained the names of the next-of-kin, and dialed the first number I found. The woman who answered was Donna Paltz, the daughter of Mrs. Rita Altman, the killer's first victim. I identified myself and told her that while I was not in law enforcement, I had some experience solving homicides and was working with the Denver Police Department. I told her there is a suspicion her mother's death was not natural, and the police may investigate. I didn't tell her it was my suspicion only, not the Denver PD, and that it was my guess the PD would eventually investigate. "Oh, my God! What do they think happened?'

"I don't know. If you don't mind, I just have one question to ask you. Did your mother ever tell you that she was fearful of someone living at Mervin Gardens?"

There was a long pause. "I don't think I should be talking to you. Why are you interested in my mother's death? Are you an insurance investigator? Is that what this is all about?"

"Look, Mrs. Paltz, I'm a friend of one of your mother's neighbors. She asked me to look into the numerous deaths at Mervin Gardens because she knows I've had success solving other homicides." I repeated my question.

After a moment, she said: "My mother was," she paused, searching for a word, "uneasy about several people living there. But she never gave me their names."

"What made her uneasy?"

"Well, one woman lingered in the lobby for long periods of time. Just sat there, watching people come and go, trying to engage them in conversation. It annoyed my mother."

My first thought was that the neighbor was probably just a lonely old lady, trying to socialize with anyone who was willing. "Did she ever threaten your mother?" I asked.

"No, Mother never said that. The woman just made her feel uncomfortable."

"Was there anyone else?"

"There was another neighbor she tried to avoid."

"Why?"

"She just said she was a nasty woman and kind of sneaky, always showing up somewhere by surprise."

"Why was it a surprise?"

"Because she wasn't expected. She was handicapped and confined to a wheel-chair."

I thanked her and hung up, thinking Carlos would eventually question her and relatives of the other four victims. He'd be asking the same questions and we could compare notes down the road. Then I thought about her description of a woman in a wheel chair. Could that be Margrette Tripp, the lady who wished me "happy hunting" in my so-called investigation? Because of her disability, I quickly dismissed her as a possible suspect. I studied my notebook and dialed another number.

Dennis Morgan was listed as the son of Arlene Morgan, who was found drowned in the indoor pool on April 25. He lived in northwest Wyoming and answered on the fourth ring. Again I identified myself as friend of his mother's neighbor and told him I was looking into his mother's death.

"What for?" he asked brusquely. "She drowned accidentally, didn't she? That's what we were told."

"There's some suspicion it wasn't accidental, Mr. Morgan. May I ask you a few questions?"

"Are you a cop, a detective?"

"No, but I've assisted the Denver PD occasionally."

"So why I should I talk to you? I'll talk to the Denver police, if and when they call."

The line went dead. I felt like a salesman making a cold call.

My third call was to Charlotte Crabtree, daughter of Janet Christie. She lived across town in nearby Lakewood. I listened to a recorded message and left my name and number, saying I needed to speak to her about her late mother. I offered no other details, hoping she would call me back.

The setting sun was flirting with the front range of the Rockies when I made my fourth and last call to Dr. Andrew Barringer, son of Dr. Russell

Barringer who died February 2 of a heart attack. The son was a respiratory specialist and I didn't expect him to answer the phone himself. As expected, I wound up speaking to a receptionist or assistant in his office. Getting him to return my call, I knew, would be tricky. I decided to be direct.

"Please ask him to call me," I said. "It concerns his father's death. It's urgent."

Sidney Luft, the fifth and last person to die this year at Mervin Gardens, had no surviving family members. He listed Leah Lamont as his personal representative and his sole heir.

I looked again at the second note the killer had delivered to me. Reading it a second time only made me madder and more determined to involve myself. Making the calls to some of the victims' relatives was like opening a valve that released some of the pressure that was building within me. At least, I felt, I'd gotten serious about finding the killer, and I had a few leads.

It was time to bring Carlos on board.

Stuffing the second note into my jacket pocket, I climbed out of my car and marched back into the old police HQ building. Sgt. Barney Cassidy looked at me over his reading glasses, perched on the end of his ruddy nose. "Did you forget something, Izzy?"

"Sort of. Is Detective Collins still around?"

"Yeah. Go on up."

I climbed a flight of stairs and found Carlos at his desk, rifling through some papers. "Back so quickly? What's up?"

"I just found this in my car in your parking lot," I said, pulling the second note from my pocket.

Again using only a thumb and forefinger, he took the sheet of paper from my hand and laid it flat on his desk, and then read it quickly. "So the perp knew you were here? This one is printed by hand. All caps."

"He must have followed me here and decided to write the note impulsively." I heard the anger in my voice, but also the hint of a slight quiver.

The last time I felt threatened was in North Korea. That was more than sixty years ago and I was a young, innocent Marine infantryman. Fate was good to me and I came home without a scratch, thanks to the quick thinking of Sam

Goodman, my lifelong buddy. Years later, Sam was beaten to death in a LoDo alley by a college student who misidentified him for his mother's lover. I solved the murder. Now I'm an old codger, not-so-innocent, and hardly fit to protect myself against a determined killer.

"Okay, Izzy," Carlos said, "here's what I want you to do. I know this will be hard, but you need to detach yourself completely. Go about your regular business. Concentrate on your club and your shows there. Think about Anita. Forget about Leah. And just let me handle it. Got it?"

I knew he was right. His advice was smart and he was thinking of me. He had my safety in mind. I felt a rush of love for this young man who was not even a relative. "Yeah, I hear you, Carlos," I said softly.

"Good. Now go home or go to Anita and try to relax. I'm on top of this now. It's first on my case list."

"Do you have any ideas?"

"I might have."

"Do you have a security camera in the parking lot? Maybe you can spot the guy sticking the note through the partially-opened window of my car."

"For crying out loud, Izzy, please stop. It's Denver PD business now, so back off."

"I'm sorry, Carlos." I knew that backing off would be hard to do. Since I solved my first homicide years ago, the thrill of hunting killers has gotten into my blood. This case apparently was a *series of homicides,* and it was now personal.

Nevertheless, I followed his advice and drove home slowly. Knowing that Anita was seeing clients in her office all afternoon, I didn't want to disturb her, much less alarm her even more so. At my condo, I parked my car in the underground garage, rode the elevator to my sixth floor apartment, and was greeted warmly by George. I don't know if he sensed my anxiety, but it seemed to me that he offered an extra large dose of loving. He had been alone for hours, so I put on the leash he fetched from the hall closet and took him downstairs for a nature break and a bit of exercise around the neighborhood.

My condo was one of the first high-rise residential buildings that went up in the district they call the Golden Triangle. It gets its name because the area is bounded by several major arteries forming a triangle on the edge of downtown Denver. The building was constructed by my late friend, Sam Goodman, who had gained a deserved reputation as a highly-ethical developer. Over the years, many more apartment buildings were built and quickly occupied by people attracted to its convenient location—close to the many downtown office buildings and cultural attractions within walking distance. The owners were largely retired elderly couples, widows or widowers who wanted to be near the action, and by younger working people earning wages high enough to afford the expensive units.

Anita and I have enjoyed visiting the Denver Art Museum, where we viewed some fabulous exhibits, like a rare collection of Monet's impressionism assembled from around the world. We also viewed the striking works of the Colorado artist, Clyfford Still, in the adjacent museum that bears his name. Considered one the most important painters of the 20th century, his life had been shrouded in mystery and most of his work hidden from the public for thirty years until his widow gave his collection of more than 3,000 pieces to the city of Denver for permanent display. He was among the first Abstract Expressionist artists who developed a powerful new approach to painting after World War II.

Also close by are the Colorado History Museum, a wonderful place that displays memorable events in the state's growth, and the Denver Center for Performing Arts, where we regularly attended popular road productions like *The Book of Mormon* and *The Phantom of the Opera*.

The day's activities left me a bit tired so when George and I got back to my place I was ready for a short nap. The bed felt cozy and I was asleep within minutes. I must have slept about a half-hour when the phone woke me. It was Anita, calling to tell me that she just learned from Leah that funeral arrangements had been completed for Sydney Luft. Services would be held later in the week at a local funeral parlor. His cremated remains would be interred in a family plot in a Chicago cemetery followed by a reception in Leah's apartment. She knew I would attend the reception, but she expected me to attend the service also out of respect for Sidney.

My first instinct was to tell her my time would be better spent investigating the murders, but then I remembered the promise I made to her and my last conversation with Carlos. So I assured her, somewhat reluctantly, that I would attend poor Sydney's funeral. Then she invited me to her house for a home-cooked meal that evening. I accepted immediately because I felt too tired to eat out. Besides, she doesn't mind that I bring George with me when we're dining alone.

Our telephone conversation over, I pondered the prospect of returning to bed to extend my nap. That decision was made for me when the phone rang again. This time is was Carlos.

"I just finished looking at the film from our surveillance camera in the parking lot," he said. "Thought you'd be interested to know what I learned."

"Well, are you going to tell me or do I have to come down there and beat it out of you?"

"I'm shaking in my boots," Carlos said. "So here's what the film shows. Someone wearing a hoodie approaches your car and slips the sheet of paper through the window and watches it drop to the seat. Then he or she turns and walks away, out of camera range."

"You said 'he or she.' You can't tell if it's a man or a woman?"

"Like I said the perp was wearing a hoodie. No face or hair was visible."

"Damn!" I muttered. "So the film tells us nothing."

"Not exactly. We're still examining it. There's something else—real evidence. Mervin Gardens Security gave us a film recorded at the pool the night Mrs. Morgan drowned. It shows her struggling with someone in a hoodie on the concrete apron adjoining the pool. Chairs are scattered all around. The person in the hoodie pushes her into the pool. Mrs. Morgan struggles to get out, but the attacker keeps pushing her back in until she's exhausted and she drowns."

"Wow! That's incredible! You've got film of a homicide being committed. Can you identify her attacker?"

"Not with the hoodie. It looks like we may have a serial killer on our hands."

***

That evening Anita treated me to a tasty repast of Southern fried chicken, corn on the cob and a colorful and crispy salad. Already stuffed, I accepted a slice of warmed peach pie topped with a scoop of Rocky Road chocolate ice cream. I had to open my belt a notch to make room. Only after the dishes were placed in the dishwasher and we were seated on the loveseat did I update her on the day's events involving the Mervin Gardens murders, beginning with the admission that Leah's suspicions were correct.

Anita leaned toward me and clutched my arm. "What convinced you, Izzy?"

Reluctantly, I told her about the second note and the surveillance film.

She threw her arms around my neck and clung to me. "Dear lord, the killer is *stalking* you, Izzy!"

"Apparently."

She pushed me away and glared at me. "Don't be so casual. This is serious." I thought she was going to cry, but then she said: "What did you mean, '*you* and Carlos have a serial killer on your hands?' You're not involved in the investigation, are you?"

"No, sweetheart, this is Carlos's case. He's just keeping me informed."

This was only partially true. Up until I interviewed the Mervin Gardens business manager and security officer, and a few victims' relatives, I had done nothing that could be considered furthering the investigation.

"Carlos needs to find a way to reduce the number of suspects. Eighteen is simply too many," I complained.

Anita remained silent for minute. "I have an idea. Sidney has no family. He left everything to Leah, including the responsibility for organizing his funeral after his death. She was going to have a private service at a nearby church, just his closest friends. But what if Leah were to hold a larger service and a reception? She'd encourage everyone in the building to come and participate. At the reception, they'd be invited to offer their own memories of Sidney—a series of eulogies at a catered reception in her apartment. You and I and Carlos would arrive early and stay late, observing everyone who came and making note of what everyone, especially the women, had to say about Sidney, and their overall behavior and demeanor. That way, you might eliminate the most obvious people from your list. After the party, Leah could tell us who the 'no shows' were. In the end you and Carlos might narrow the list to a reasonable number."

Right there and then, I fell in love with her for the umpteenth time. Or maybe it was just her mind that I loved. Oh, I love her smile and her body and her humor and her cooking and everything else about her, but her mind was something special. "That's a great idea," I said, stammering slightly. "Do you think Leah would agree to it?"

"Why not? She's the one who first insisted there was a serial killer in her building. Anything that would identify him...." Her point made clear, she left the sentence unfinished. "I'll call her right now."

Within minutes, Leah had agreed to start the planning.

I left Anita's place early, went home and retrieved the full list of occupants in Leah's building. Somewhere on that list, I was convinced, was the murderer.

I dialed another number on the list of relatives. The HOA business manager had identified Mrs. Christie's surviving sister, Charlotte Crabtree. When the sister answered, I realized I was talking to a really old person. She spoke with a tremor in her voice and was hard of hearing. I had to repeat myself several times. I introduced myself and told why I was calling. When she didn't say she'd already spoken to the Denver police, Carlos especially, I began asking a few questions.

"I understand your sister was unmarried?"

"Yes, she was engaged many years ago, but he broke it off," she stammered. "She became disillusioned with men and remained single the rest of her life. But she found joy in animals, always had a pet and enjoyed going to concerts. Despite her age—she was 89--she was an outgoing person and had many friends where she lived."

"Did she ever have an ugly incident with any of her neighbors?"

"Only once, which is why she remembered it—because it was so unusual."

"How so?"

"It was a woman who lived downstairs from her. One day she came upstairs and banged on my sister's door. She complained about her dog. She said the dog was always barking, loud and for long periods of time. That was not true. Janet's dog was a gentile little cocker spaniel with a very sweet disposition, and very quiet. The neighbor was nasty, full of anger, very threatening, which was alarming—and in a way bizarre."

"Why was that?"

"We didn't think she was capable of threatening anybody. She was always in a wheelchair."

Of course, I immediately thought of Margrett Tripp. Several other people had mentioned a woman in a wheelchair. There were two residents who depended on wheelchairs at Mervin Gardens. The other was Mrs. Louise Flowers, in her late '60s, a widow living on the top floor. Unlike Mrs. Tripp, she was seen leaving her chair occasionally. But neither one seemed capable of sprinting away from my club, much less committing murder.

I looked again at the list of other occupants and randomly selected two names. They were simply hunches and the first was one I couldn't ignore, only because of his name—Bradley Rothkiller. Now if ever there was a candidate for suspicion, Bradley was it. Go ahead and laugh if you want to, but stranger things have happened in murder mysteries. So buckle up Mr. Bradley Rothkiller, I said to myself, because here I come.

It turned out that Bradley lived on the first floor with a pit bull who snarled at me when his master opened the door a crack to observe me while I observed him. He appeared to be about 60 and fit for his age. What loss of hair he suffered on top, he made up for it with a luxurious black beard and mustache streaked with ribbons of gray. I introduced myself as a friend of Leah and wondered if he could spare me a minute to talk about the recent deaths in their building.

His expression was a mixture of confusion, followed by hesitation, followed by curiosity.

"What's there to talk about?" he said with a somewhat croaky voice, while nudging his dog away from the door.

"The police are looking into ther deaths" I said. "They suspect foul play and your neighbor, Leah Lamont, is quite frightened. Since I've solved several homicides I told her I'd look into it."

"Are you a detective?" he asked with a dubious look.

"Hardly. I'm a professional performer, a stand-up comic.Murder investigations are more like a hobby," I said, chuckling.

He didn't see the humor. "That's an odd hobby for a man your age."

"I agree. It gives me something to do when I'm not performing."

"Let me put Dempsey in his kennel, then you can come in."

A moment later I was sitting on a purple sofa facing Mr. Rothkiller who sat in a cream-colored recliner. He was wearing a gray sweat suit and white tennis shoes.

"Your dog is named Dempsey? Like the boxer?"

Mr. Rothkiller permitted himself a sly smile. "Yeah, my dad followed boxing and Jack Dempsey was his hero. For some reason this dog reminded me of my father so that's what I named him, kind of in his memory."

"Very nice," I said, feeling some success at

gaining his acceptance. He seemed ready to talk about the deaths.

"One of the deceased was your neighbor, Dr. Russell Barringer. I see he lived down the hall from you in Apartment 109. What can you tell me about him?"

"I thought he died of a heart attack?"

"That was the preliminary finding, but it's being reviewed."

"Really? So the police suspect someone did him in, eh? Now that's a surprise. He was a quiet man, a retired shrink with a bad heart," suddenly revealing a West Canadian accent. "He minded his own business."

"How about you? Were you a friend?"

"Not really, he kept his distance. He was leery of dogs, especially Dempsey. Said he was bitten once by a pit bull."

"Do you know anyone living here who was mad enough to kill him?"

"You want me to point a finger at someone? Hey, I may be from Alberta but I'm no fool. If you want to find a killer, you figure it out." He rose from his recliner and showed me to the door.

I stood in the hallway outside his apartment and thought: *Mr. Rothkiller didn't want to implicate anyone, but he implicated himself. All he had to do was sic his dog on old Barringer with the bad heart and he could have induced a heart attack.*

I looked at the second name I had selected and headed for the third floor and apartment 301. It was at the end of the hall. A small table stood outside the door. Atop the table was a straw basket containing an assortment of small ceramic animals—rabbits, squirrels, frogs and a white-tailed fox. The brass nameplate on the door read: Cynthia Cavendish. I rang the bell.

The woman who answered the door was petite and white-haired. She wore a pink sweater over a black shirt and a black skirt, and clutched the kind of cane blind people use to feel their way around. "May I help you?" she said in a soft voice.

The cane was an immediate put-off. With impaired vision, why should I expect her to be a helpful source? I asked myself. Then I thought, *Don't be so hastily judgmental, Izzy. Her hearing seems okay, so maybe she heard something that might be helpful.* I introduced myself and soon found myself sitting in her living room, surrounded by another assortment of animals, stuffed, and much larger than her hallway display.

"You like animals, "I said. "Why don't you keep a real one, a friendly dog or cat?"

"I've thought about it. The animal would have to be trained for a blind person. I understand they're really amazing—the things they can do. I've procrastinated, but I might opt for one, yet." After a pause, she said: "What can I do for you?"

"Your next door neighbor, Rita Altman, died last January. If you can recall, did you hear anything out of the ordinary involving her? An argument or anything strange?"

"Well, that's a long time ago and my memory is not what it used to be." She thought for a moment, then said: "I'm afraid I can't help you. I don't remember anything unusual happening."

"That's okay, Mrs. Cavendish. Should you recall anything later on, I'd appreciate a call."

I gave her my card and left.

Standing in the hallway outside her apartment, I felt the heavy weight of hopelessness. The last two interviews had produced nothing promising.

I hoped Carlos had better luck.

TEN

RAMBLING AROUND MY APARTMENT that evening, the phrase *serial killer* suddenly resonated in my mind. Carlos had mouthed the phrase earlier. It now repeated itself like the ticking of a clock. *Serial killer. Serial killer. Serial killer.* I recalled the helter-skelter days of the 1970s and '80s when names like Ted Bundy, John Wayne Gacy and David "Son of Sam" Berkowitz made headlines. But the term seemed to have passed from my consciousness since then. Why?

A few minutes at my computer gave me the answer. The number of serial killers, I learned on the internet, dropped 85 percent the last three decades. A recent report from the FBI said that serial killers now account for fewer than one percent of killings, probably because of longer prison terms and a reduction in parole so convicted murderers are less likely to kill again.

I continued searching the internet.

There were more reasons serial killings had plunged. There was less hitch-hiking today than in the past and more helicopter parents keeping an eagle eye on their kids. And more security cameras everywhere—about 60 million of them! And then I came across a curious fact. Even as the number of serial killings dropped, the number of murders solved also plunged—from 91 percent in 1965 to about 60 percent today.

"*Oy gevalt!*" I muttered aloud, and then thought: *Killers are now getting away with murder about 40 percent of the time! Like whoever's been murdering the folks at Mervin Gardens.*

I continued to search the internet and learned that there have been over 200,000 unsolved murders since 1980. How many of those should be attributed to serial killers? No one knows. Holy cow, I thought, I've really got my hands full on this case. Then I reminded myself that it's all in Carlos's hands, not mine, although I've resisted letting go despite my promises to Anita and Carlos. Surely Carlos knows what he's up against. Or does he?

On impulse I called him and started questioning him about what I'd just learned.

He didn't respond to my questions. Instead, he said, "Izzy, are you kidding me?"

"What do you mean?"

"You'retestingmyknowledge,"hesaidaccusingly.
" Like I'm some kind of rookie detective. Shame
on you."

"You're right, Carlos. I'm sorry. I was searching
the internet and I couldn't believe what I was
reading. I just had to check it out with you. For
example, did you know that about a third of all
serial killers did so for enjoyment?"

"Yes, and for lust, thrills or power," he replied,
offering specifics. "And another third—30 percent
to be exact—do it for financial reward."

"So you're on top of these facts?"

"We get the reports as soon as they're released
from various databases. The chief will call a
meeting to discuss the stats if he feels they're
relevant to any current investigations."

"Will he call a meeting about the Mervin Garden
murders?"

"Maybe. Anything else you want to ask me,
Izzy? I hope not 'cuz I'm really busy."

"No, that's all, Carlos. Again, I apologize. Thanks
for your patience."

Anita called to remind me that Sidney's funeral

would be held next week, followed by the reception at her apartment. The last thing I wanted to do was attend another funeral. I'd been going to too many lately, people I'd known for years. My list of friends was shrinking, and it saddened me when I thought about it. I was making new friends, younger friends because they were less likely to die on me. But Anita was going to Sidney's funeral to support Leah. In fact, she was arranging it and the reception that would follow, and knew I'd be there. Maybe the killer would be there, screw up, and drop a clue.

***

On the day of the funeral, the rain started falling about 7 a.m. and by 11 a.m., when I arrived at Anita's place, there were city-streams in the curbs and people rushing under umbrellas to their destinations. Anita was waiting for me in her doorway and jumped into my car. Ten minutes later we were at Mervin Gardens, where Anita went up to Leah's apartment to fetch her. Fifteen minutes later, we were at a small church near midtown.

I sat with Anita in the third row and watched a

crowd of about 80 people arrive and take a seat in the darkened chapel. I scanned the crowd for any familiar faces and quickly recognized Sidney's pool pals, and a few of his other neighbors I had seen occasionally in his building's courtyard. I also saw several of his friends I had met when Anita and I went out to dinner with him and Leah. Then I saw the two ladies in the wheelchairs. Mrs. Flowers' chair was positioned in an aisle. Mrs. Tripp had stationed her chair near the back of the chapel.

The pastor delivered a short eulogy, based on information Leah had given him about Sidney. His message was laden with clichés and hardly portrayed the essence of the man. It was a generic talk, one that he'd probably delivered dozens of times. After listening to some equally generic music, the clergyman announced that Sidney's ashes would be flown to Chicago for burial in a family plot. With that the service ended and the gathering was invited to go Leah's home where lunch would be served.

When the crowd had assembled in her apartment, Leah invited Anita and me to sit with her. Carlos joined us.

I sat with Anita and took notes about who was sitting together and their general demeanor. Carlos sat next to Leah. Later, while they were eating a dessert of raspberry sherbet and cookies, Leah announced that anyone who desired could share their stories about Sidney, but first she would speak about his life.

For the next few minutes, she displayed re-markable composure while she talked about his growing up in a suburb of Chicago, of attending dental school and starting his practice. She mentioned his late wife briefly, noting they never had children, and that he'd retired early and moved to Colorado. She met him when he bought a condo in their building at Mervin Gardens. Only at this point did she falter, sobbing quietly and briefly. Everyone waited respectfully. Her comments completed, she invited the others to share their memories.

A silver-haired woman wearing a pink blouse and charcoal gray slacks said she lived on the same floor as Sidney and will always remember him as a good neighbor. She admitted she had a crush on him—"I'm sorry, Leah"—and told a story about his coming to her door one evening to borrow a cup of sugar and she was so flustered she gave him flour instead. The line drew laughter. I wrote it down.

Another woman rose, somewhat unsteadily. Holding onto the chair, she said she wanted everyone to know how kind Sidney was to her. "When I had my hip surgery, he was the first to come by and offer to do my shopping. He helped me around my place, doing little things to make life a bit easier. I simply cannot understand why anyone would want to...." She stifled a cry and sat down. The lady in the wheelchair, Margrette Tripp, recalled that Sidney sometimes went to the liquor store to buy her favorite wines. "We'd have cheese and crackers and chat for awhile," she said. "He was a gentle man."

Several more people rose to offer complementary comments, all of them women except for a tall, slender man in a dark blue polo shirt and tan slacks. He drew admiring glances from the ladies. "Hello, my friends," he addressed them, not bothering to introduce himself. Apparently he felt it unnecessary since they all seemed to know him. Except me.

"Who is that?" I whispered to Leah.

"Godfrey Stage," she whispered back.

Stage spoke for about three or four minutes, describing how he first met Sidney on the tennis court. He recalled the hours they played together, then cooled off with a few beers in the lounge. "I'll miss beating him," he said with a laugh before seating himself.

Another woman stood up and introduced herself as Ida Sanders "for those who don't know me." She launched into a meandering tale about how she'd helped Sidney decorate his apartment when he first moved in. "He had no idea what to do," she said. "We had such fun selecting things." Then her demeanor changed. "I don't think he ever appreciated all that I had done for him."

The eulogies over, Mrs. Tripp rolled up to our table.

"Hello, Mrs. Tripp," I said.

"Oh, you remembered me?"

"Yes, indeed, how are you?"

"A lot better than poor Sidney," she blurted.

I shot a quick glance at Leah, but she seemed oblivious. Anita, on the other hand looked furious.

When Mrs. Tripp left, Leah, Anita, Carlos and I reviewed the eulogies for any information that would be helpful to our investigation. We especially sought to eliminate possible suspects.

"What do you think, Carlos?" I asked. "Did we learn anything useful?"

"From a police standpoint, not much," he said, scratching his chin. "We can eliminate the women in the wheelchairs and those who use walkers, but we knew that already. "And we could probably drop a few who just didn't seem capable. We might look into those who expressed anger. All in all, not very promising."

I had to agree, although I was intrigued by some of Sidney's former neighbors like Mrs. Tripp. Anita whispered to me: "That woman was incredibly insensitive."

Indeed she was, I thought. It made me wonder what else is there to learn about Sidney's former neighbors. Perhaps I should resume my interviews.

ELEVEN

AFTER CARLOS LEFT, LEAH invited Anita and me to stay longer. I accepted immediately, hoping to acquire more knowledge about Sidney and his past. We sat in her living room and I remained silent while the women chatted. When the conversation turned to Sidney, I saw my chance to ask a few questions.

"When did you and Sidney first meet?" I asked Leah.

"About two years ago," she replied. "He had just moved in. We have a custom in our building to welcome newcomers with a coffee. It was my turn to host the event. About twenty residents attended, almost everyone in the building."

"As the newest occupant, what sort of an impression did he create?"

"He was very nice. As you know, Sidney was quite handsome. It took only a few words of conversation to realize he was also charming. All the women in the building noticed, especially the single ones."

"A good-looking man who was unattached," I said. "Yes, I can see why he would attract attention. Were any of the single women especially forward in their behavior?"

"Do you mean did any of the girls come on to him like it was their last meal?"

I had to suppress a laugh. Leah was such a straight shooter. She didn't mince words.

"Yes, that's what I mean."

"You mean besides me?"

This time I couldn't restrain myself. I laughed out loud while thinking that I needed to find room in my gig for her humor. "So, you found him attractive, too?" I said it with a smile on my face.

"Of course I did, Izzy. But I didn't fall all over him like some of the girls did."

I mused over the fact that despite their ages, older women continued to refer to themselves as "girls." Did old farts like me call each other "boys?" I didn't think so but I supposed some of them did.

As we talked, I learned that Sidney had at times been a hotel manager, financial adviser, clothing model and actor in community theater. He was a fitness nut, working out four days a week in the Mervin Gardens gym and visiting the pool almost daily during the summer. He had acquired a magnificent tan from face to toes that he proudly displayed in his navy blue swim trunks with white stripes, or his lime Speedo with orange stripes. When he climbed out of the pool, his trim torso gleaming in the sun, all eyes it seemed, turned toward him.

"If he had so many admirers," I asked Leah, "why would anyone want to do him in?"

"Jealousy!" Leah shot back. "If they couldn't have him, nobody would."

"That's insane, isn't it?" I asked.

"Aren't all serial killers insane?" she countered.

Anita had witnessed my questioning routine in previous homicide cases and said, "Izzy, I know what you're doing. You promised me you'd leave this case to Carlos. Stop this questioning right now. We should go."

"Okay, but let me remind you it was your idea to enlarge the reception gathering. I'm just following up on that."

Anita frowned, then said, "I know, I just wish you'd let Carlos handle it. We know the killer is a very dangerous person. I worry about you."

"I appreciate your concern, honey, but let's face it. I can't just walk away. An unsolved murder festers in my *kishkes* like a virus. I've got to treat it or it'll get worse. I have a plan that might solve these murders and I'll need your help. Are you in?"

She looked at me like I was a lost soul. "Izzy, I just don't want anything to happen to you."

"With your help, nothing will. You're my partner, and I know that between us—and Carlos, too—we'll figure this out. How about it? Are you with me?"

She threw her arms around my neck and kissed me. "Yes, I'm with you. But I don't know what I'm going to do with you."

***

I took Anita to her house and told her I was going back to Mervin Gardens in the hope of interviewing at least one more resident. In the meanwhile, I asked her, if she would do some research. "See what you can find online about any of the other residents." If skepticism were water, her expression would have drowned me in seconds. "No, seriously," I said, "you never know what you might find. Okay?"

"All right,," she said, reluctantly. "Be careful."

I headed back to Mervin Gardens, parked my car, and checked the list of residents that Leah had provided me. I scanned the list and randomly selected a name for no other reason that it kind of intrigued me. I knew I was playing poker with a lousy hand. It cases like that, you just play the cards you've been dealt and hope for the best. I took the elevator to the fourth floor and rang the doorbell at apartment 409 occupied by Mr. and Mrs. Zbigniew Pulasky.

The man who opened the door may have been the largest man I'd ever seen face to face. I guessed his height at near seven feet tall and his weight about 350 pounds, the size of a lineman in professional football. He wore only a sleeveless undershirt and baggy gray pants. His feet were anchored in a pair of tattered black slippers.

"What you sell I already got," he said in a heavy Eastern European accent, "or I don't want."

But he said it with an easy smile that signaled he was not going to slam the door in my face, and that he was willing to engage in some conversation. Maybe I was the only person he might converse with that day, other than his wife. That thought often occurred to the elderly residents of places like Mervin Gardens.

I took his demeanor as an invitation to start a conversation so I introduced myself as Leah Lamont's friend and a part-time homicide investigator. The idea must have intrigued him because he invited me inside, waited until I had seated myself, then offered me a shot of vodka.

I accepted, knowing that to decline would be impolite and probably jeopardize any conversation.

Drink in hand, I asked him if he knew any of the people in the building who had died that year. He thought for a minute and said, "Dat nice lady across the hall. She die in March, I think."

I tested my memory. The only death in March was Janet Christie, 89, spleen and liver failure, according to the original coroner's report. I had already spoken to her daughter.

"Was that Mrs. Christie?" I asked.

His face lit up in recognition. "Ya, dat one. Nice lady," he repeated himself. "Big surprise, she die."

"Why was that?"

"Very old lady, but very healthy. She walk every day. Drive car. Go shopping. Go to church every Sunday and have people come for coffee almost every week. Very, how you say, social?"

"Did you know any of the other people who died this year?"

""Only dat gentleman, Mister Luft. I in dis country only short distance. Know few people."

"Did you know anyone who would want to harm Mrs. Christie?"

He shook his massive head decisively. "Na, she was—"

"A nice lady," I said, interrupting him.

"Ya, like my Elena," he said. The mention of his wife made me wonder if she was at home.

"Is she here?"

As if on cue, a woman emerged from a bedroom and joined us in the living room.

"Dis Elena," her husband said. "She talk better

English than I talk."

Elena was an elegant-looking woman, perhaps 10 years younger than her husband. She wore black slacks and a white turtleneck sweater. The only make-up I could discern was a touch of lipstick. She offered her hand, slender and soft, with beautifully manicured French nails. "I hope you and the police catch Sidney's killer," she said, speaking softly and with only a hint of European inflection.

"Did you know him well?" I asked.

"Only as a neighbor," she said, but her eyes conveyed a somewhat regretful look as did her expression.

Her appearance was a striking contrast compared to her husband. If ever there was a seemingly mismatched couple, I thought, these two filled the bill. Her husband attempted to be sociable. He offered me another shot of vodka, but this time I declined. I left their apartment wondering about the state of their marriage. And whether or not Elena had the hots for Sidney.

***

After a light supper, I slid into the desk chair at

my computer and resumed searching the internet for more information about serial killers. More surprising facts started jumping out at me. I grabbed a yellow pad and began making notes.

- Serial killings account for no more than one percent of all murders committed in the U.S. Based on the 15,000 murders committed annually, that means no more than 150 are committed by serial killers.
- The FBI estimates there are between 25 and 50 serial killers operating throughout the U.S. at any given time.
- If there are 50, then each of them is responsible for an average of three murders a year.
- About 17 percent of all serial homicides are committed by women.
- Serial killers span all racial and ethnic groups.
- Many serial killers appear to be non-threatening, normal members of society. Because they can appear to be so innocuous, they are often overlooked by law enforcement officials, as well as their own families and friends.
- Most serial killers have well-defined geographic areas of operation—a comfort zone in which

they are likely to stalk and kill their prey—*like a single building in Mervin Gardens!*

- A popular misconception is that most serial killers are either mentally ill or are brilliant but demented geniuses. Neither is true. They are much more likely to exhibit antisocial personality disorders such as sociopathy or psychopathy, not considered mental illnesses by the American Psychiatric Association.

- Contrary to popular perception, it is not high intelligence that makes serial killers successful. Instead, it is obsession, meticulous planning and a cold-blooded, often psychopathic personality, that accounts for their murders.

I re-read the notes I had scribbled on my pad. There was a lot there I never knew before. My eyes went back to the fourth item on the list: *About 17 percent of all homicides are committed by women.* I recalled what Leah had said about motivation—a woman's jealousy may have been the reason Sidney Luft's ashes were now on their way to burial in the family plot.

So was there one woman who had lusted for Sidney, besides Leah? One woman with anti-social behavior traits who lived in Mervin Gardens, who was capable of meticulous planning and cold-blooded murder? I had a chance to match those questions with the actual occupants when Anita called later that night .

"I know it's late, but I just finished my internet research of Leah's neighbors. Do you want to hear it?"

"Absolutely," I blurted. "Anything juicy?"

"Well, I wouldn't call it that, but some things I discovered are interesting. I don't know helpful they are. That's for you to decide. You're the detective."

TWELVE

DURING THE EIGHT DECADES I've spent on this rotating globe called Earth, I've learned a few things about human nature.

First, in order to live a happy life, a person must find something to do, someone or something to love and, finally, always have something to look forward to. Second, don't let expectations dictate your life; there will always be disappointments. Third, first impressions are overrated.

In my "happy life" formula, I recall many years past when men found joy in their jobs, women found fulfillment in marriage, raising children and being the glue that kept the family together. Today, women also work either out of necessity or because they simply want to. Since they still keep house and raise the children, they've added to their interests, but also their burden. Statistics show that married men live longer than those who never marry. And yet many men will tell you they are happier now that they're divorced or separated. For companionship they settle for dogs or other animals they love.

Both men and women live happier lives if they always have something planned—a movie, a concert, a sporting event, a dinner, an adventurous trip or travel with a group. We love the excitement of anticipation.

Unhappy people are usually frustrated people whose expectations are unmet, and they've been unable to adjust. So they live out their lives in anger or feeling sorry for themselves. We see these people everywhere. Lonely, sad people, without friends.

And, finally, first impressions are often misleading. Notorious serial killer Ted Bundy was seemingly charming to people he first met. Adolph Hitler mesmerized millions of Germans with his charismatic demeanor and grand promises to make Germany great again. So-called "nice" girls can become wild and passionate tigresses in bed to the delight of their husbands or lovers.

I knew little about the occupants of the Mervin Gardens building where the serial killings occurred except for the measly details I'd learned from Leah, the business manager, the security guard and the couple of residents I'd talked to. I needed to speak to more of the occupants. That would take lots of time and effort. I didn't even know where all the deceased were found or who found them, but I could obtain that information with less trouble.

I called Carlos and put the question to him.

"You promised to lay off this case, Izzy." His tone was neither impatient nor encouraging, just matter-of-fact. I think he was resolved that I couldn't help myself, so he should stop expecting me to keep my promises.

"I know, but just get me that information and I won't bug you anymore. I know you've got it in your reports." After a moment of silence, he said, "Hang on." I heard him rifle through papers.

I drummed my fingers on my desk while I waited. I already knew that Sidney was found in his bed by a Security Patrol officer. Leah had asked him to make a security check because she couldn't reach him. And Arlene Morgan was found in the Mervin Gardens pool by another Security Patrol officer making a grounds check. I had no idea where the other bodies were discovered or by whom.

"Okay, here's what you asked for," Carlos said. "Rita Altman was found on the floor of her bedroom by her daughter. Dr. Barringer was found sprawled in his recliner by a neighbor who was expecting him to visit that night."

"What do you mean 'sprawled?'"

"Apparently he was trying to get out of his recliner but couldn't quite make it. His legs and most of his body were on the floor but his head, chest, shoulders, arms and hands were still in the chair."

"What was the neighbor's name?

Carlos game me a name and phone number. I made a note.

"And Mrs. Christie?" I asked. She was the oldest victim and the one who'd lived there the longest.

"Yeah. She was found in bed by her daughter, Charlotte Crabtree. She had not talked to her mother for several days. She said they were in the habit of speaking every day as her mother's health began to deteriorate so she decided to come by. The door was locked and when she didn't respond to the knock, she used a spare key to enter." Carlos paused a moment, then said: "That's it, Izzy. That's all of 'em. Gotta go."

Who can I call? I glanced at my little notebook with the name of the neighbor who found Dr. Barringer. His name was Derek Stark. I called him and invited myself over. I was greeted by a short, rotund man with a boyish face crowned by a mass of red hair.

I got right to the point. "Mr. Stark, I understand you found your neighbor, Dr. Barringer, the day he died."

"No, you mean my brother, Derek. My name is Dylan." He called his brother. Derek came out of a bedroom and I thought I was seeing double. The brothers were identical twins, looking like two jolly little elves with pink cheeks, short arms and legs, and impish grins.

"How well did you know Dr. Barringer," I asked them.

"As well as anybody living in the building," Derek said.

"Probably more so," Dylan said. "I think he enjoyed our company."

"We'd spend evenings talking about opera and

science," Derek said. "Not everyone here was willing, or able, to do that."

"How did you happen to find him that night," I asked.

"We were expecting him to come by for a glass of wine and some talk, our usual routine. When he didn't show up, I knocked on his door and, when he didn't answer it, I tried the door and found it open. I went inside and found him on the floor by his recliner. He looked like he was getting out of it when he died. His upper body was on the floor but his lower body was on the footrest, like he fell forward."

"And you called 911?"

"Yes. They arrived within minutes, examined him, and said he was dead. Later, we all learned he had a heart attack."

"Not necessarily," I said. "The police think he was murdered. Do you know anyone here in the building who might do that?"

The brothers looked at each like they'd just heard the most astonishing question in their lives.

"Murdered? How horrible," Derek said, framing his face with chubby hands.

"How terrible!" Dylan said, emulating his brother's gesture.

I waited for them to answer my question. Finally, Derek said, "Why would anyone do that? The doc was a gentle man."

"Did he have many friends here?" I asked.

Dylan replied: "No, he was selective about making friends. A little bit of a private person. But no one, that I knew, ever said anything nasty about him."

After leaving the Starks' apartment, I called Mrs. Christie's daughter and left a message.

***

That evening I continued my research about serial killers. I came across an article addressing the question: What makes a serial killer? The author, a qualified sociologist and criminologist, suggested that it was a combination of genetics and experience. He said that certain genes can predispose people to violence and that one gene, in particular, called the *warrior* gene, is present in about 30 percent of the population. That statistic caught my attention. *Yikes! Almost one out of three people.* They can be spotted because of their aggressive behavior.

Another common thread among serial killers was that they experienced childhood trauma or early separation from their mothers. Consequently, they learned to suppress empathy or suffered damage to areas of the brain that affected emotional impulses. They often suffered humiliating rejection and grew up fearing and hating people, and became loners.

If I had a suspect or two I could match their personalities against this profile.

But, so far, I had no idea who the killer might be. This case was growing more difficult than the others I'd solved. I was beginning to feel a bit overwhelmed. George sensed my mood and squeezed between my knees so I could stroke him while he licked my hand. He knew how to comfort me, even if only temporarily.

I had been in bed for an hour, unable to sleep, when a question popped into my head. Did these victims have anything in common that might point to the killer? It's such an obvious question! Why didn't I think of that earlier? I need to focus on that, I told myself.

THIRTEEN

IT WAS SATURDAY NIGHT and the Izzy Brand Comedy Club in downtown Denver was already nearly filled with customers when I arrived. Danny was energized by the crowd. I love Danny like the son I never had. He's always wanted to be a stand-up so I've kind of become his mentor. He does occasional gigs at the club but shies away from going on the road. He's a home boy. Despite my age, I occasionally will do a gig out of state— just to keep up with changing trends. Anita goes with me when her client schedule permits it.

My gig was sandwiched, as it always is, between the opener and the closer. The opening act tonight was a skinny gal from Chicago with enough tattoos of Chicago's skyline to decorate all the chairs in the front row. She had an edgy voice and an awkward demeanor. Her jokes were topical and occasionally cutting, but with an aw-shucks semi-apology typical of Chicagoans who wear a small-town outlook in a big city suit. The Generation Xers in the audience loved it, the boomers not so much. She got a decent hand when she finished.

I had studied the crowd from the wing. A mixed audience. About half were regulars, old-timers who came about twice a month to hear my stories aimed at the older crowd. Tonight there was a nice sprinkling of younger people. I like to see that. Sometimes I feel that stand-up comedy is a dying art, appreciated only by folks my age. But when the kids come out—that's anyone under the age of fifty—I get pumped up. As long as they keep coming, stand-up will survive. I should aim some jokes in their direction. But first I've got to acknowledge the old farts that came out.

An elderly couple went to their doctor for an annual exam. After the man's exam, the doctor said: "You appear to be in good health. Do you have any medical concerns you would like to ask me about?"

"In fact, I do," said the old man. "After I have sex with my wife, I feel cold and chilly, but then after I have sex with her a second time, I'm hot and sweaty."

After examining the man's wife, the doctor said: "Everything appears to be fine. Do you have any medical concerns you would like to discuss with me?"

The lady replied that she had no questions or concerns.

The doctor said: "Well, your husband has an unusual concern. He claims that he's usually cold and chilly after having sex with you and then he is hot and sweaty after the second time. Do you know why?"

"That's because the first time is in January, and the second time is in August."

After the laughter died down, I continued.

Speaking of getting old, are you having trouble keeping up with today's technology? It's changing my life. I woke up at 2 a.m. to go to the bathroom and just had to check my email before going back to bed. Yesterday, I tried to enter my password on my microwave, then I turned off the modem and got this awful feeling that I just pulled the plug on a loved one.

The laughs kept coming.

What do Jewish people do on Christmas? Since all other restaurants are closed, they go to a Chinese restaurant. This is the year 5,780 in the

Jewish calendar and about 4,780 in the Chinese calendar. That means the Jews suffered about a thousand years without Chinese food.

I had one more joke for the old-timers.

Failed marriages are a lot like algebra. Have you ever looked at your X and wondered Y?

It was time to acknowledge the "kids" in the audience.

Maybe you're thinking about getting married. I read that 4,153,237 people got married last year. Not to cause any trouble, but shouldn't that be an even number?

When wearing a bikini, women reveal 90 percent of their body. Men are so polite they look only at the covered parts.

This being a presidential election year you should know that every vote matters. America is a country where its citizens will cross the ocean to fight for democracy but won't cross the street to vote.

My gig over, I hung around to catch the closer. He was in his late twenties and dressed like a preppy from Princeton. He'd attracted a lot of attention on the East Coast and was making his debut in the West. Would this newly hip town accept his style? He played it safe. Instead of pure humor, he chose to be the professor and educate the audience.

In the 1400s a law was passed in England that said a man was allowed to beat his wife with a stick no thicker than his thumb. Hence, we have "the rule of thumb.

Many years ago in Scotland, a new game was invented. It was ruled "Gentlemen Only, Ladies Forbidden." Thus the world GOLF entered the English language. The crowd began to get a bit restless. A voice boomed: "This ain't the Ivy League. Tell us some jokes!"

"Okay, I hear you," he said. "Just one more fact. Which day generates more collect calls than any day of the year?"

"Father's Day!" a young woman shouted out. "But that's a really old joke. It's no longer relevant. We all have cell phones—and unlimited calling."

The crowd laughed and the preppy comic looked distraught and lost. I wondered how he'd made to the ranks of closers. In desperation, he took off his brown sports coat with the leather patches on the elbows, rolled up the sleeves on his button-down blue shirt, and loosened his yellow tie. His jaw set, he leaned toward the audience, and began a story.

John and his friend, Shawn, lived in Denver and decided to go fishing in Montana. They loaded a van and headed north until they got caught in a terrible storm. So they pulled into a farm and asked the attractive lady who answered the door if they could spend the night.

"I realize it's terrible weather out there," she said, "and I have this large house to myself, but I'm recently widowed and I'm afraid what my neighbors will say if I let you stay in the house.

"Don't worry," said John, who prided himself for being a gentleman, "we'll be happy to sleep in the barn and, if the weather breaks, we'll be gone at first light."

The lady agreed and the two men found their way to the barn and settled in for the night.

Come morning, the weather had cleared and they went on their way. They enjoyed a great weekend of fishing, but about nine months later John got an unexpected letter from an attorney in Montana, representing the attractive widow he and Shawn had met on their fishing trip.

He called his friend and asked, "Do you remember that good-looking widow at the farm we stayed at on our fishing trip about nine months ago?"

"Yes, I do," said Shawn."

"Did you get up in the middle of the night to pay her a visit?"

"Well, um, yes I did," Shawn said, embarrassed about being found out.

"And did you happen to give her my name instead of yours?"

"I'm sorry buddy, I'm afraid I did. Why do you ask?"

"She just died and left me everything."

The audience howled. Preppy-boy grinned and wiped his moist brow. He straightened his shoulders and went into a fast-paced routine of one-liners, like Rodney Dangerfield, drawing applause.

He was going to be okay, I thought, and started for the exit before he finished.

As I approached the door I noticed a figure

leaving. The person was wearing baggy pants and a hoodie that obscured his face. Or was it a woman? The figure had the build of a small man, but with wider hips. The hoodie obscured the chest so that I could not tell if the person had a bosom.

Still, I felt strongly it was a woman. I recalled that Carlos also had concluded that the hooded figure in the parking lot was a woman.

She's still stalking me!

I walked quickly, trying to catch up to her, but she noticed me behind her and began sprinting. I could not keep up. She turned the corner at the next block and disappeared. I stopped to catch my breath. In those next few moments I decided hereafter to concentrate on the female occupants in the Mervin Gardens building where Leah lived because I felt certain the serial killer was a woman living in that building. Back in my apartment later that evening, I retrieved the list of occupants Leah had given me and highlighted all the females. They outnumbered the men 18 to seven.

I had my work cut out for me.

When I retrieved my Sunday paper outside my

door the next morning, an envelope slipped out of the paper. I opened it and found a typewritten note. It read:

If you continue to run around as you are doing, you old fool, it will certainly be the death of you.

That clinches it, I thought. Not only did the note confirm that the person I saw last night was the perp who was stalking me, but she was taunting me. She was cocky and self-assured. And willing to take risks. I made a mental note of those characteristics.

***

The morning paper carried a disturbing story. It seems a new virus had broken out in China and medical scientists feared an outbreak there could spread around the world. The Chinese were, as usual, being tight-lipped about the details, but other sources said the virus had begun in a market and spread throughout the region. What concerned American health officials was that thousands of possibly infected Chinese had entered the U.S. in recent weeks, probably spreading the disease wherever they went. Didn't we just go through this recently? I thought. Ebola. And something called

SARS? Well, with those experiences behind us, surely we were prepared for this new scourge, weren't we?

I put the paper away and turned my thoughts to the murders in Leah's building. I was convinced that she was correct in her suspicions, that someone was killing her neighbors and that the perp, according to my recent experience and Carlos, was a woman. Based on what little evidence I could muster, the serial killer thought she was invincible, so much so that she had started stalking me and taunting me with mocking letters. Was she a narcissist? Was that another personality trait that might identify her? Possibly, but I needed a lot more evidence. Real evidence, I thought.

Now that Carlos was also convinced that the Denver PD had a serial killer at large, I wondered if he had acquired any new evidence. I called him and put the question to him.

"Nada," he said, "zilch. But if she showed up at your club last night, I'll check the security cameras in the area. You've got some cameras in your club, too, don't you?"

"I'm not sure. I'll have to check with Danny."

"Well, if you don't, it's high time you installed a few." He sounded like a teacher lecturing a lagging pupil. I knew Anita would get a kick out of that. We normally have a late Saturday night snack after my gig, but not last night. She'd told me she was tired and would be going home right after my show. She knew nothing about the perp coming to the club, so I called her in the morning.

FOURTEEN

ANITA ANSWERED ON THE third ring. "I'm sorry I couldn't join you for dinner last night," she said. "I didn't have much of an appetite."

"That's okay, hon. I didn't eat, anyway. I had a surprise visitor at the club and she grabbed my attention."

"Who was that?"

"The serial killer."

"Izzy, is this a joke?"

"No, I'm serious. She was wearing a hoodie, but I when I followed her outside she started running. I couldn't keep up. Anita, she's playing games with me. I told Carlos and he's going to look at the security cameras in the area and at the club, if we have any. He scolded me in advance in case we don't."

"Let me know if he finds anything," said with an urgency in her voice.

"I will, hon."

After she hung up I resumed my research about

serial killers. I read about a character in Flannery O'Connor's *A Good Man Is Hard to Find*. The character is a misguided escaped prisoner who stumbles upon a family after their car crashes on a trip to Florida. He orders the other prisoners who escaped with him to systematically murder all the members of the family, including the grandmother. Before she dies, he discusses his personal philosophies with her. First he insists he is innocent of the crime that put him jail. Because his conviction was a mistake, he calls himself The Misfit. He has no spiritual beliefs so he relies on himself to be his own moral compass. He questions the meaning of life and has examined his own experiences to make sense of his current situation. He has a steady view of life and acts according to what he believes is right. He forms rudimentary philosophies, such as "no pleasure but meanness" and "the crime don't matter."

I put the book down, feeling sad and dejected. How awful, I thought, to know there were monsters like that in the world. But that was fiction, I reminded myself. O'Connor made up the Misfit character. He wasn't real. And yet, I knew that O'Connor was a perceptive observer of human behavior. She most certainly modeled her Misfit on someone who actually existed. How did that pertain to the Mervin Gardens' serial killer? Was she a "Misfit" living secretly among Leah's neighbors? And could he and Anita identify anyone who would match those descriptions?

My thoughts turned again to the serial killer. I was really not much closer to identifying her—I had convinced myself it was a woman—than I'd been since the beginning of my investigation. If only I could find something, anything, that linked the victims. The only things they seemed to have in common were that they were elderly and all lived in the same building. I reminded myself that Carlos was on the case. I wondered how he would proceed.

First, he would gather information about the victims. Now that he's convinced the murderer is a serial killer, he would try to determine if the killer had a special reason for choosing her victims. Was there a connection among them? He'd talk to their neighbors, friends, relatives. And that's what I've been doing. Carlos would want to know if the victims had any enemies—a question I've been asking. Or if they were afraid of anyone in the building, or had been threatened. I've asked those questions, too.

Izzy, old boy, you've been going by the book. I began to feel better about my approach.

George interrupted my thoughts by fetching his leash from the hallway closet and dragging it to me. It reminded me that I hadn't taken him outside since early in the morning. George has his routine. He'd stop in the lobby of my condo apartment building to visit briefly with Walter, the doorman who usually had a treat in his pocket, then head out the front door for a snappy walk along Speer Boulevard. Finding a grassy spot, he'd do his business and then wait while I retrieved it with a plastic bag.

While walking back to our building I was greeted by the woman in the wheelchair, who lived in the same building as Leah. Since that building was about a mile from mine, I wondered how she got to my neighborhood. I doubted that she rolled herself here. That question was answered when she told me she had taken a bus to shop at a store she liked in my neighborhood. We chatted briefly before George started tugging his leash, letting me know he was bored with the conversation and wanted to sniff a few more trees before returning home.

Before leaving, I said: "Forgive me, but I can't recall your name."

"It's Tripp, Margrette Tripp."

"Oh, yes, now I remember. Nice to see you again, Miss Tripp."

"It's *Mrs.* Tripp," she said, speaking in clearly enunciated, if clipped, syllables. I lost my husband six years ago."

"I'm sorry to hear that. Goodbye."

"Happy hunting."

"What do you mean," I asked.

"Your investigation, of course. Everyone in the building knows you're looking for a murderer. You are, aren't you?"

Other than the woman who was stalking me, I didn't realize that my efforts had become common knowledge. Mrs. Tripp was waiting for my answer.

I ignored her question. I wasn't going to have a

conversation about my investigation. "Have a nice day, Mrs. Tripp." I left the lobby and got into my car, still thinking about my encounter with Mrs. Tripp.

Something about it buzzed around in my head, but I couldn't identify it. It wasn't anything she said, nor was it her appearance. And yet, I felt I was missing something that was important. I've had this sort of experience before and it taught me not to belabor the thought, that the missing piece would reveal itself eventually. With that comforting assurance, I put it out of my mind and replaced it with Rebecca's problem. I hoped Mike Halloran would get my message and call me shortly. My wish was quickly granted.

My landline was ringing as I entered my apartment. Mike and I exchanged some chit-chat before he asked me about the job I had in mind. I told him about Rebecca's problem. I didn't have to give him too many details before he said: "Okay, I get the picture. I'll need his home and work addresses. I should have a report for you in about a week."

***

While I waited for Halloran's report on Rebecca's husband and Leah's plans for the funeral reception, I realized I had time to work on my next gig at the club. I pulled out my files of old jokes and started to review them. They struck me as a bit stale and not in tune with our current world. I had established a habit of recording the dates I used each joke. Glancing at the dates, I was surprised by how often I'd been telling the same stories. I really needed to introduce some fresh material. I picked up a pen and pad, slid into my recliner and let my mind wander.

FIFTEEN

WRITING COMEDY AIN'T EASY, as any joke writer will tell you. It helps to work with others. Then, you can feed off each other. One guy will start a story and wait for the others to finish it. That's why TV shows hire a team to write for comedy series. Comic movies often use a team of writers, too. Top comics may have a stable of writers, too. Me? I work alone.

My recliner is where I do my best creating. I start with some meditation where I breathe deeply and try to feel the oxygen passing through my body while putting everything else out of mind. They call it "mindful breathing." This relaxes the body and leaves your mind open to fresh ideas.

Coming up with ideas might seem easy, but actually shaping them into jokes that will produce laughs is hard work. I learned that lesson early in my career when a lot of my stuff simply bombed. I didn't know what it took to be successful, that is, create a routine that has the audience laughing from start to finish. The average stand-up gets four to six laughs a minute from the audience. When I first started it seemed an eternity before I got my first laugh. There were times I was so dejected, I wanted to just walk off the stage. But I kept at it and finally got the hang of it. I learned the fundamental of comedy writing. I use my personal experiences a lot. My lifestyle and habits come into play and my fans know who I am and what my values are. The more personal, the better. I approach comedy writing like a story. Who are the characters? Where's the setting? What's the situation or conflict?

The most important parts of my set are the beginning and ending. My opening lines will establish the tone, help win over my audience. I save my best joke for the end. Throughout, I try to keep my routine conversational—just friends getting together and having a good time.

Stand-up comedy has its roots in vaudeville. In the old days, performers used props and lots of sight gags. It was called *slapstick*. One of the best performers to bridge vaudeville and stand-up comedy was the late, great Jerry Lewis, especially when he teamed with Dean Martin. Just seeing them on stage often drew laughs, even before they said a word. Slowly, the vaudeville acts dispensed with slapstick and focused on telling stories, anecdotes, material taken from the performers' own life experiences. The more a performer revealed about himself, the more the audience liked him. And, if the audience *loved* you, you could tell them almost anything and make them laugh.

I often think about the great ones of the past— Groucho Marks, Jack Benny, George Burns, Milton Berle, Bob Hope, Rodney Dangerfield, Bill Cosby, Red Skelton, Red Buttons, Sid Caesar, and those fabulous gals, Lucille Ball and Carol Burnett, who led the way for more female performers. I know there are some fine comics out there today, but I don't think they have the flair of the old-timers. Well, that's my opinion anyway.

We call a complete routine a *set*. It's structured like a story—a beginning, a middle and an end. The length of a set depends on whether you're doing the opening act or the headliner. If you're the featured act, you could be on stage for an hour or more. That requires lots of jokes to be a headliner—in top clubs in New York, Chicago, LA and Dallas. I almost had my own TV show years ago, but they rejected me. Said I was too *ethnic*. I told them at the time that's like saying Bill Cosby was too black.

These days I do the opening act or the middle act, unless the closer is a no-show. In that case, I stand in for him or her. It rarely happens. But, just in case it does I have a variety of sets, 20 minutes as the opener, 40 minutes as the middler, or an hour as the closer.

After my opening lines, I follow with more jokes, or *bits* as we call them. I detail the characters and the situations they're in. Every bit has a punchline—the conclusion—which is the funniest part of the joke and is almost always a surprise, something the audience didn't expect.

To create a smooth flow, I use *transitions*. These are short, conversational bridges that connect one joke to another. And, finally, I finish my set with a *closer*. This is the final joke in the show, maybe the best in my routine. It leaves the audience howling as you say goodnight.

So, what new jokes can I write tonight?

Husband and wife scenarios usually make for good comedy. The trick is to find the right platform—nothing too nasty or too sugary. Anita and I are not married so I can't tell personal stories. Besides, I'm not comfortable putting her in my routine. For some strange reason I'd been thinking about the role of the alphabet in comedy the last few days. Have no idea why.

Maybe my muse was telling me to combine the elements. Let's see: wife/husband/alphabet. What can I do with that?

I mulled several ideas. I thought about the scene in the show, *Fiddler on the Roof,* when Tevya asks his wife, *Do you love me?* It triggered an idea.

My friend Jake and his wife, Selma, finished dinner and Selma says to her husband: "How come you never tell me how you feel about me?"

"Feel about you? We've been married 25 years. That should tell you how I feel."

"But you never say it," Selma says. "You never put it into words. I don't know what you think."

Jake pauses for a minute, and then says. "Let's go through the alphabet. A is for Adorable, B is

for Beautiful, C is for Cuddly, D is for Delightful."
He continues until he stops after Honeybunch.

"What about I, J and K?" she asks.

"They stand for I'm Just Kidding."

I wrote the joke on an index card and resumed thinking about another one, something on a timely subject. How about religion? This led me to a transition. I could say that there was a time we avoided telling jokes about religion and politics, but times have changed. So have people's views about those subjects. Religion, especially, has seen quite a bit of relaxed rules, maybe because fewer people are going to a house of worship. I mused over that subject for awhile. *What if a Catholic church and a Jewish synagogue, both in the same neighborhood, were having trouble filling their pews? Father O'Brian and Rabbi Rabinowitz meet and commiserate. What can we do to keep open? they ask each other.*

"I have an idea," the rabbi says. "What if we combine our congregations and conduct ecumenical services? A little bit Catholic, a little bit Hebrew? We alternate the location, Saturdays at my synagogue, Sundays at your church."

"Sounds good," Father O'Brian says. "We always begin our services with a singing of Ave Maria. Is that okay?"

The rabbi strokes his beard. Finally, he says: "No problem. Just one little adjustment. We sing Oy vey, Maria.'"

Another transition, another joke. "Among my friends is a woman who is younger than most of us. The other day we were talking about health insurance. Most of us are eligible for Medicare, but she's not. She's too young. "So are you covered?" someone asked her. "Yeah," I said, she's got Kindercare."

The gag writing session made me tired. I turned on the TV to catch the news before going to bed. The newscaster was giving an update about the virus that had erupted in China and was making its way around the globe. Health experts warned it could be a problem in the U.S. if it ever crossed our shores. "Just what the world needs," I thought to myself.

SIXTEEN

AFTER EATING A HEAVY lunch, neither Anita nor I had much of an appetite for dinner. Instead of going out, she came over to my place and I fixed us a light supper of vichyssoise soup and a small salad. A gourmet cook I'm not but I can whip up a tasty snack like that any time. I never bothered to take any cooking classes or memorize too many menus after my wife passed away, but I enjoy a good meal as much as the next guy. Living alone, I just can't bring myself to cook elaborate dinners for myself. It's only when Anita joins me that I regret not being able to place a sumptuous feast in front of her.

She was clearing the table when Mike Halloran called.

"Just got the report on your niece's husband," he said. "I'll skip the smaller stuff and get to the core."

"Go ahead."

"Malcolm has a boyfriend in Queens."

"Malcolm is gay?"

"Yeah, they've had a relationship for years. When he's not at home with your niece, he's with Brandon Baker, a choreographer in Manhattan. Apparently, that's where he's been for the last three weeks, including the six days we were watching him. We've got more stuff on both of them. Do you want it?"

"No, that's enough for now. Thanks, Mike. You did good work. Send me a bill."

"This one's on the house, Izzy. You bailed me out a bunch when we were in school. Maybe down the road I'll ask for a favor."

Anita had stopped putting dishes in the sink when she heard me say "gay." She was looking at me with that blank expression she assumed when she heard something that might surprise most people. It was part of her professional demeanor, I assumed.

"Well, now you have a logical explanation," she said. "He couldn't bring himself to tell Rebecca."

"He's a louse," I blurted. "I have no sympathy for him. He should've been more forthright. In fact, he shouldn't have married her to begin with.

What a farce! Now, he'll be forced to be honest—after treating her so miserably."

"You're being pretty judgmental, Izzy."

"Darn right, I am. She's my niece. She deserves better. I'm very angry at him."

SEVENTEEN

THE NEWS ON TELEVISION that night was bad for the world and the country. National health officials were reporting that the virus from China had infected several thousand Chinese and killed several hundred. They were alarmed that the virus was spreading outside China and would soon reach the United States, if it hadn't already. There was no vaccine to kill it. Cautionary steps were being advised. Facial masks, social distancing and frequent hand-washing were strongly advised.

The news was certain to spook some people, I thought. I remembered the polio scare back in the 'forties when parents watched their neighbors' kids come down with it, fearing it would soon strike their own children. And, ultimately, it often did. Those were hard times—to see once-healthy children reduced to crippled youngsters. What most of us didn't know was that FDR, our own president, also was a victim of polio, a fact kept from the public until after he died.

The virus aside, I had other bad news to deal

with. I had to tell my niece why her husband had been acting so cold to her. I didn't relish being the messenger. But she had confided in me. I needed to tell her what I'd learned. This was not the kind of news you tell someone by a text message, an e-mail or even a telephone call. I wanted to tell her in person, but she was in Manhattan. I had no choice but to phone her. I would have liked Anita to listen in, but I knew she wouldn't do it. It would violate her ethics. So I made up my mind to pay close attention to Rebecca's reaction, then discuss it with Anita if she was willing.

I dialed Rebecca's number.

She was surprisingly restrained when I told her. "Well, that explains a lot," she said, matter-of-factly. "I should have known. He certainly gave me enough clues."

I didn't ask her any questions, but I assumed she was talking about the nature of their love-making, or lack of, and not having any children.

"I'm such a fool, such an idiot," she said. "I thought he and Brandon were just friends. They've known each other since high school. I suspected that Brandon was gay, but I never dreamed that

Malcolm . . . Oh, God!" For a moment I thought she was going to sob, but she didn't. She's one tough cookie, I thought.

"What are you going to do?" I asked.

"Obviously our marriage is over. I'll petition for a divorce. Mom will be more upset than me. She really likes Malcolm."

"Is there anything I can do, honey?"

"No, you've already helped a lot."

I wished her luck and asked her to stay in touch.

"Of course I will, Uncle Izzy. Thank you for all you've done."

***

The next morning, I called Leah to talk about the service for Sidney. I wanted to hear more about her reaction to the comments the others made.

"It was interesting to see who was sitting together," she said. "I don't know that it was helpful finding the killer."

"Probably not," I said. "Serial killers don't have partners. They work alone. Did you see or hear anything out of the ordinary?"

"No," she answered. "As I said yesterday, people

were polite and discreet. Well, everyone except that guy who criticized Sidney's tennis partner. I never heard Sidney complain about him so I don't know what to make of that."

"It doesn't appear to have anything to do with Sidney's death so I'd ignore it," I told her. "What about that Sanders woman? She seemed almost angry when talking about him. Did you think she was a bit out of line?"

"Oh, she's like that. No one pays much attention to what she says."

Perhaps not, I thought, but that's what makes a serial killer so hard to catch.

***

Late in the afternoon, Carlos called me with information that would significantly impact our investigation. He had ordered Sidney's body exhumed and an autopsy performed. He now had a preliminary toxicology report. "Leah's friend was poisoned," he informed me.

" Can you give me any details?" I asked.

"As I said, the report is preliminary. More tests by the medical examiner are underway. But it seems Sidney inhaled or digested ricin, according to the coroner's office."

I'd heard of ricin but didn't know much about it. At my request, Carlos filled me in. "Ricin is a poison found naturally in caster beans," he said. "If chewed or swallowed, they can cause injury or even death. Ricin can be made into a powder or mist. Based on evidence we found in his lungs, the coroner thinks Mr. Luft inhaled it. At this point we don't know how, why or when. But now we're going to exhume all the bodies and do more autopsies. The coroner is enlisting additional staff, reluctantly because it's gonna blow his budget. It'll be interesting to see what they find."

"Do you suppose the victims gathered together at one point and infected each other? After all, they all lived in the same building."

"No, ricin poisoning is not contagious. The illness can't spread from person to person through casual contact. Ricin works by getting inside the cells of a person's body and preventing the cells from making the proteins they need. Without the proteins, cells die. Eventually, this is harmful to the whole body. If not treated early, the person will die."

"What about symptoms?" I asked.

"Depends on how the victim absorbed the ricin. If ingested, he would likely develop vomiting and diarrhea, severe dehydration, low blood pressure and even more serious symptoms like liver, spleen or kidney failure. But Sidney apparently *inhaled* the poison. That would make breathing difficult. He'd be sweating and feel a tightness in his chest, among other things."

"A lot of things puzzle me, Carlos, and one of them is this: how did the killer get Sidney to inhale the poison?"

"Good question. I'm only guessing, but I think she may have concocted some kind of spray to create a mist and somehow exposed him to it. For example, she may sprayed around him."

"But then she would have exposed herself, too."

"Not necessarily—if she had been careful to avoid the spray."

Then I wondered if Leah was aware that Sidney had any of the symptoms? It was a question I had to ask her.

EIGHTEEN

"POISONED? OH, MY GOD!" Leah gasped. "You mean it wasn't accidental? That someone deliberately *poisoned* him?"

"I'm afraid it's true," I said softly.

"Who would do such a horrible thing?"

"That's what I'm going to find out, Leah. I promise I will."

I didn't know exactly how I would find out. Only once before had I investigated a murder involving poison, but I may be over my head this time. I'll have to work closely with Carlos since he has access to proceedings and information not available to me, like the autopsies he's ordered. Those autopsies will make it interesting to learn the real cause of death of the others. But first I had to ask Leah some questions. I told her what Carlos had told me—that Sidney apparently inhaled ricin in powder form, or in a mist. Did she know where or when that might have happened?

"Not when we were together," she said. "I don't recall his being exposed to any kind of powder or mist." She paused, then said, "oh my god, if he was exposed while with me, then I was exposed, too! Am I in danger, Izzy?"

"Have you had any symptoms? How are you feeling?"

"No, I'm feeling fine"

"I think you'll be okay. Had you been exposed, you'd know by now." I didn't tell her that death can take place within 36 to 72 hours of exposure.

***

Now that Carlos had learned that at least one of the deaths was attributed to poison, I felt I should so some research and learn more about employing poisons as a murder weapon. I called him, but he was not at his desk so I left a message. My next option was the Internet, that depository of sometimes useless information, where I often went to find answers to my questions. Of course, you have to be able to separate the facts from the nonsense. Too often conspiracy theorists will use the Internet as a platform to preach outlandish ideas. I found a website written by a professional toxicologist who did exhaustive research and cited the sources of all his information. That was a clue that I could depend on his information to be accurate.

The author of the article wrote a fascinating history of murder-by-poison. He noted, for example, the nineteenth century is sometimes called the golden age of poisoners because in the early 1800s scientists had not figured out how to detect a poison in the corpse. It wasn't until 1840 that the first test for arsenic became available. It took another thirty years to detect cyanide, nicotine and morphine. And poisons were easily available, including arsenic that can mimic a natural illness. It was a time when killers could get away with murder while scientists were trying to catch up.

Things changed in the twentieth century when forensics started removing politics and putting science into pathology. In the early 1920s, the average family medicine cabinet included radioactive radium, thallium and morphine among common household products—a treasure trove of poisons. New York City's chief medical examiner began classifying death investigations according to the chemical found in corpses through toxicology tests, thus eliminating natural deaths or those caused by accident. After that, they started catching murderers. Another authoritative article said that most killers are convinced they can get away with murder-by-poison. They are careful plotters and they think of themselves as being extremely clever, smarter than the police.

My research online was interrupted by a phone call from Carlos. "I got your message. What's up?"

"Tell me more about killers who use poison."

"Don't you have a gig you have to prepare for?"

"I'm caught up. Please indulge me, *boychek.*" Over the years I've introduced him to many Yiddish words. I feel it's a necessary part of his education.

After a pause, he said, "They're often perceived as being among the coldest killers."

"Why is that?"

"Because their murders are always pre-meditated, never by impulse. They have to pick the poison so they research it and then plan how to use it on their victim. That takes time, so they spend days or weeks thinking how this is going to go. And they watch as their victims eat or drink the poison or, as in Sidney's case, inhale it. They're very methodical."

I told him that I had read that the public believes most murders caused by poison are perpetrated by women.

"Actually, six out of ten poisoners are male. But men also use a gun to commit about nine out of ten homicides. That seems to suggest that a greater number of poisoners are women than in other types of homicides."

Okay, I thought, another reason to believe the Mervin Gardens killer was a woman. "Let's talk about serial killers in general. What about motive? What makes them different from other killers?"

"Good question, Izzy. I've been looking at that myself. Here are the most frequent reasons: Anger. Thrill-seeking. Financial gain. Attention-seeking. They're all self-explanatory, right? Gotta go. See ya."

I had made notes as he spoke. "Mucho thanks, kid. See ya."

He had spat out the motives in short and punchy words. I should focus on them, I told myself. If

I could learn the reason *why* someone poisoned Luft—and possibly the others—I would have a leg up on finding the killer. I looked at Carlos' list of motives. You don't think of elderly people as seeking thrills. Financial gain? Don't think so. The folks living at Mervin Gardens are all well-to-do—wealthy widows or divorcees with substantial settlements. Or that immigrant, Zbigneiu Pulasky, a world-champion weightlifter and entrepreneur who brought a fortune to America. Lonely elders commonly seek attention. Would they draw attention to themselves by doing away with a neighbor? And what about *anger?* Was the killer so mad at so many people that she methodically went about selecting a poison to do them in?

I needed to answer those questions. Somewhere in those answers I will find the killer. I flipped open my pad and studied the list of victims again. I noticed that Arlene Morgan, who was found supposedly drowned in the pool, had a surviving brother. He lived nearby, in Aurora, the largest Colorado city outside Denver. Rather than phone, I decided to drive to his house and question him there. Twenty-five minutes later, I pulled up to the curb in front of his home in a cul-de-sac. The two-story house in a tree-lined neighborhood had white bricks and black shutters. A large cottonwood guarded the front entrance.

Wallace Dillon answered the door wearing a short-sleeved shirt and tan walking shorts. I gave my name and again identified myself as a friend of his mother's neighbor and as a local performer and occasional helper to the Denver PD. He stood in the door, processing the information. It was a lot, I knew, and I waited while he sorted it out.

After a few moments, he said, "And what can I do for you?"

"There is reason to believe your mother's drowning was not accidental," I said, adding that her cause of death was premeditated.

"You mean she was killed? "

"Possibly."

I was still standing in his doorway. He looked beyond me to the street and to his neighbors' houses. "Come in," he said.

He led me into a living room and motioned me to a sofa.

"Who is it?" a woman's voice asked from the

kitchen. In a moment, a middle-aged woman wearing a yellow dress joined us.

Dillon introduced me. "This is my wife. Mr. Brand thinks Mom didn't drown by accident, that she was murdered."

The woman put a hand to her mouth as if to stifle a scream or a cry. She moved to stand by her husband and put an arm around him.

"I can't go into details at this point," I told them. "An investigation is underway. May I ask you a few questions?"

"What do you want to know?" Dillon said.

"Did your mother ever express fear about any of her neighbors?"

Dillon looked at his wife.

"The busy-body," she said.

"Oh, yeah. She told us about a really nosy neighbor who was always asking questions. One day she learned my mom was having a dinner guest and she wanted to know who the guest was. Mom told her: 'If I wanted you to know, I'd tell you.' The woman became furious and accused my mother of being rude. Mom told her she was a nosy pain in the ass. Mom didn't mince words.

The woman threatened her."

"In what way?"

"Just said that she'd be sorry."

"Did she give you her neighbor's name?"

"No. But she said the neighbor was in a wheelchair."

I left the Dillon house thinking about Margrette Tripp. Several people had pointed a finger at her for her angry outbursts. But she was disabled, confined to a wheel-chair. The perp I had in mind was physically fit—enough to race away from me at my club.

At this point, I still didn't have a viable suspect.

NINETEEN

THE NEXT EVENING, ANITA and I went to dinner at a new restaurant south of the city. It was at her suggestion because the restaurant featured Thai food, one of her favorites. I told her to order for both of us. She selected the popular *pad thai* and said the portion would be large enough to share. She was right. The server brought us a steaming bowl of rice noodles stir-fried in a hot wok with onions, egg, bean sprouts and shrimp. Anita said the concoction was tossed in a sweet-sour-salty sauce made from tamarind, fish sauce, chilies, and lime juice. Crushed peanuts were offered as a garnish.

As we ate, I told her about my conversation with Rebecca, and my surprise how calmly she accepted the news that her husband of ten years was gay. "I thought she would be more emotional, maybe even hysterical. But she wasn't."

"She was probably exercising extreme self-control. You don't know what happened after talking to her."

"You're right. I can only try to imagine what a woman would think or do after hearing such news. I don't know anyone who went through that experience. Do you?"

"Yes, I've had several clients—women who've come to me for help in dealing with the situation. I learned what they were feeling. Their reactions were varied. Some were very upset, to put it mildly. They felt betrayed. It was a word they used often in our conversations. They meant they were led to believe they were marrying a straight man, not a homosexual. They also used the word 'deceived.' Those wives were so angry they could hardly speak. One told me she would ruin—her actual word—her husband. Their divorce was nasty. He lost his well-paying job and is now working far below his qualifications, and earning a lot less pay."

"That seems silly of her," I said. "How could he afford the alimony?"

"She didn't care. She earned more than he did. Their kids were grown up and she didn't need it."

"And the other women? The ones who were more...reasonable?"

"There was only one other. She displayed remarkable sympathy for her husband. She said his life must have very unhappy, being attracted to men while living with a woman he didn't love. She actually felt sorry for him. Fortunately, they had no children."

"And she had no clue he was gay when they married?"

"She recalled that he struggled to act romantic, but all he really wanted was oral sex. Looking back, she felt that society had compelled him to marry a woman, that's what was expected of him from his parents and his straight friends. They really didn't know him, how he felt. He willingly agreed to a divorce, even felt relieved."

"Then why come to you? It seems she handled it quite well without your advice."

"She wanted help in dealing with her elderly parents and friends. They couldn't understand why she didn't recognize that he was gay early on."

I remained silent, trying to process what she had told me.

She helped me out by adding: "Rebecca

displayed enormous emotional stability when you told her. She's probably gone through a range of emotions since then—anywhere from tremendous anger to ultimate acceptance, depending on her personality. Is she the kind of person who absolutely collapses at being dealt a severe emotional blow, or one who picks herself up and moves on? You're her uncle, Izzy. What do you think she will do"

It was a question I was asking myself. "She's always been resilient. I think she'll be all right.".

***

During the following week, more autopsies were performed. When they were all concluded, Carlos invited me down to Denver PD headquarters to review the reports with me.

"All the deaths were attributed to poison," he said, "but not all of them employed ricin. Other poisons were used."

"What does that tell you?" I asked.

"The killer likes to experiment, to use a variety of methods."

I didn't reply, but my mind was telling me much more. I pictured a killer who was toying with the authorities—police and medical. She was convinced she was smarter and enjoyed testing their abilities. Perhaps she lost patience with poisons that took too long to kill her victims and she was searching for agents that acted more quickly. Certainly, in my mind at least, the killer was a complicated person.

I retrieved Leah's list of occupants and began to study the names again and what I had learned about them. There were twenty-four apartments in the building, all of them occupied by single people except for the immigrant couple, for a total of twenty-five occupants. Since I was convinced the killer was female, I eliminated all the men living in the building. That left 18 suspects. At first I thought this was overwhelming, a near impossibility. Then I remembered I had faced exactly the same situation before—the murders on the Danube cruise ship—when almost all the passengers were suspects. I was able to winnow that list down. That's what I needed to do now with the Mervin Gardens murders. But how?

It would have been simpler if all the murders were committed in a brief period of time. Perhaps

I could have determined who was out of town during the period, and therefore eliminated them. But the deaths occurred over a five-month period. Determining who was out of town at each death would mean interviewing every female occupant. Eighteen interviews. Not likely. There had to be another way.

Then a strange thing happened. I started getting calls from the occupants themselves, suggesting I look into this person or that one for various reasons. Perhaps they simply wanted to be excluded from my list of suspects by pointing me in another direction. On the other hand, I could not afford to overlook any possibility they might be correct. I listed their names, if they gave them. Not everyone agreed to do that. I took the names of their suspects and their reasons for naming them.

The motives given proved interesting, everything from envy, jealousy, revenge to plain-old hostility. I showed the list to Carlos and Anita. They had similar reactions.

"Par for the course," said Carlos.

"Typical," said Anita.

***

That evening, Leah prepared two lists for me. The first listed all the occupants, the second recorded the calls I had received from residents suggesting I investigate their neighbors.

"Let's look at everyone, one at a time," I suggested. "Just tell me anything that comes to mind."

For the next two hours, we sat in her living room and went through both lists. She talked in a kind of rambling manner during which she offered both objective and subjective opinions. I made notes as she spoke. She said she would eliminate certain people for myriad reasons. Some, in her opinion, were not competent to plan murder—to research and execute such a deed. Or they lacked imagination or the organization skills required. Or they were too kindly and incapable of committing murder. Or they simply would have no reason to do it. Four required walkers to get around. A fifth had been out of town, visiting a relative for a month. The list was growing smaller.

I took another tack. Thinking about motive, I asked her to rank the remaining names on a scale of 1 to 10 with regard to anger, thrill-seeking, financial reason or attention-getting. As I expected, she identified no one as a thrill-seeker, none with financial problems, several as attention-seekers, and a handful as angry. I underlined the names of the angry ones.

When it came to the second list, urging me to investigate neighbors, she displayed a range of emotions—from delight to legitimate concern, sometimes laughing aloud, other times muttering "I think they might be on to something there," or words to that effect. In the end, she concluded their tips were mostly fantasy or wishful thinking, but a few might be taken seriously. One woman, in particular, caught my attention. Her name was Dorothy Spelt. Leah said she was in her late fifties, divorced, physically fit, and had recently retired as an associate professor of psychology at the University of Northern Colorado.

"She's quite intelligent. She doesn't have many friends here. Of course, she's only lived here about two years. Even so, she's managed to alienate a number of people with her high-and-mighty attitude."

"What was her problem?"

"The laundry room. She refused to follow the rules," Leah said.

"For example?"

"Each of the five buildings has a single community laundry room containing a large washing machine and dryer. They're operated by inserting a card—no coins.We reserve our times by posting them on a bulletin board. This helps us organize our days and avoid conflicts and jams. At least it does whenever everyone obeys the rules. And everyone does, except Mrs. Spelt."

"What does she do?"

"She does her wash whenever she feels like it, even if the time has been reserved by someone else. When confronted, she says she doesn't care and calls the others 'small-minded' because they're 'slaves' to rules. Her anger is scary and she never forgets the encounter. A few times she threatened to strike another resident."

I added her name to my list of angry people

***

The late night TV offered glum news. The virus was spreading. Hospitalizations and deaths were increasing, including the first known cases in the United States. There were few suggestions from Washington, but the Center for Disease Control was advising everyone to wash their hands frequently and avoid large crowds.

TWENTY

THE NEXT MORNING, I ate breakfast quickly, walked George, and returned to my study to learn about other forms of poisoning. Fortunately, I found quite a few articles on the Internet written by academics and other professionals. For example, a Pulitzer Prize–winning professor of science journalism wrote a book about how forensics could determine whether a death was caused by murder, or not. Discussing cases where victims were poisoned over a period of time, she addressed the signs and symptoms.

Ethylene glycol, the compound in anti-freeze, she wrote, can cause kidney damage, so a victim displays the symptoms of kidney disease. Arsenic will cause a range of symptoms, from gastroenteritis to respiratory problems. Ultimately, the victim will suffer extreme sensitivity to touch in their hands and feet, and even develop skin lesions. In India there is a species of monkshead called "devil's helmet." It produces a particularly lethal seed which forensics identified, resulting in the conviction of a number of suspects. Several women planted foxglove in their gardens to produce digitalis, which can be fatal. The women put the digitalis in salads and served it to their husbands. The women were caught and sentenced to prison for long terms.

Were any of these methods used to kill other Mervin Gardens victims? I called Carlos and asked him.

"Good timing, Izzy. I just got the reports on the others." He proceeded to tell me that arsenic was used to kill Rita Altman and that ethylene glycol killed Russell Barringer and Janet Christie. And, of course, they had found ricin in Sydney Luft's body.

"What about Arlene Morgan, who drowned?"

"She was the exception. No poison. But her drowning was not accidental. We know from the security film that the perp had tussled with her before pushing her into the pool, then didn't let her get out even though she was exhausted. She finally drowned."

"Three different poisons in five victims," I said.

"Exactly. The perp liked to try different methods and was not above using brute force—as in Mrs. Morgan's case. Of course, it didn't take much effort to drown a woman of that age."

"The other deaths were made to appear natural, but the poisons induced organ failures. In Mrs. Altman's case, arsenic exacerbated her respiratory problems."

"And the others?"

"The autopsies showed they had diseases that became fatal when they were poisoned. In Barringer, the ricin triggered a heart attack. Mrs. Christie suffered from liver and spleen problems. The ethylene glycol caused their organs to fail."

"So what do you conclude from all that?"

"As I said, the murderer liked variation. She was not content to settle on one poison. Why not? Well, the most obvious answer is to hide the murder, to convince us that death was caused by a disease or illness. She was successful until the numbers started adding up, making Lamont suspicious, especially after it was her boyfriend who became the latest victim."

I thanked Carlos for the information and

hung up. I wanted to review the telephone tips I received from the occupants of Leah's building. I retrieved the pad where I had written notes of those conversations, and began studying them. A half-hour later, I had finished and concluded that almost all the so-called tips were unhelpful. They fell into two categories. One, fanciful conspiracies conceived in the minds of imaginative older citizens. For example, the man who earnestly suggested that the murderer was the strange lady on the fourth floor who had told everyone that she was once abducted by aliens. She was probably programmed to kill her neighbors, the man insisted.

And two, anger was often cited as a motive. Several callers suggested that the victims probably offended the murderer. "If you find out who was offended, you'll find your killer," a soft-spoken woman assured me. On second thought, that made sense. Carlos had also given anger as a motive. I should think about that.

Then Anita called me. She had done some searching on the internet, as I had asked, and discovered a few things of interest. A woman,

Mrs. Dorothy Warner, who lived on the sixth floor, had been arrested four years ago for assaulting another woman in a road rage episode on Route 40 in Wheat Ridge. She paid a fine and was released in consideration of her age. She was eighty-one. Another woman, Mrs. Dora Watley, was arrested for repeatedly harassing a neighbor. She was released after a judge lectured her on civil behavior. "Learn to rein in your temper," he advised her. And a man named Horace Tripp, who lived on the first floor, was killed in an auto accident on I-25 and his wife severely injured. Her name was Margrette Tripp. After she recovered she sought out the other driver and threatened him. She was arrested and released. Neighbors said she then became surly and angry "at the whole world."

I jotted down the names in my little notepad.

That evening, as I was walking George, I ran into a friend. "Did you hear about Larry Slater's wife?" he asked.

"No. What?"

"She passed away two days ago. And we can't find Larry. He's disappeared."

***

The following week attention turned to the opening of the Mervin Gardens pool. Joyfully, the pool regulars returned to their favorite adventure in the sun, claiming umbrella-shaded tables and chairs and numerous lounge and folding chairs placed on the wide concrete border around the pool. In the water, groups of elderly ladies clutched foam noodles while they clustered to exchange conversation. A few men occasionally joined them.

Their joy was short-lived. The virus had spread across the country, people were told not to congregate, to wear masks and wash their hands frequently. Finally, the Mervin Gardens Home Owners Association, following state orders, closed the pool and all other public amenities in the complex, and strongly suggested everyone stay at home. Leah and her active sun-worshiping friends were disappointed. They resigned themselves to incessant telephone conversations, hours on their computers, finally opening books they had neglected for months, and mind-boggling days staring at their television screens. One of the aging

Lotharios started to call the women, suggesting diversions. Some of them accepted. Titillating tales circulated.

All but essential businesses started closing, among them movie theatres, fitness centers, hair and nail salons and bars. With the restaurants also closed, Anita and I shared most meals at our homes. She'd cook a really nice meal, and I'd order a takeout from a favorite Chinese, Italian or Mexican eatery. I'd either have it delivered to my place or pick it up. The new lifestyle was comfortable for introverts but for extroverts like me and most of my crowd, it drove us crazy. I wandered around my apartment looking for something to do. Fortunately, I had projects.

Dealing with my niece's marital situation had taken some time for several days. Of course, searching for the serial killer consumed many hours. And now I had lots of time, especially after Danny called me to tell me he was closing the club under orders from the state. We'll do our last show on Saturday night, he informed me. "That'll be your last set until we get word to reopen. Lord only knows when that'll be."

The uncertainty left all of us feeling uneasy—Danny, the stage crew, the servers, me—we all wondered how long the shut-down would last. Danny said he'd continue to pay wages to the staff but he was concerned about how long he could carry the club without income. The comics he had lined up were also canceled at other clubs. I wondered when—and if—I would resume working. At my age, nothing was certain.

***

The club was packed for our last scheduled show. I guess people were going to make the best of it until they were forced to shelter at home.

Considering that the virus was on everyone's mind, I had no choice but to build a set around that subject. But I was going to wring every laugh out of a situation that left people feeling unhappy and anxious. After all, we all know that laughter is the best medicine.

Wearing a mask inside your home is highly recommended. Not so much to stop the virus, but to stop eating.

Finally, we've found a way to avoid annoying people. When this quarantine is over, let's not tell them.

Not to brag, but I haven't been late to anything in over five weeks.

A young mother told me it may take a village to raise a child, but it's going to take a vineyard to raise hers.

Never in a million years could I have imagined I would walk up to a bank teller wearing a mask and ask for money.

"Good show, Izzy," Anita said, clutching my arm as we left the club.

Later at her home, we focused on the serial killings. "I'm beginning to think that anger was the killer's motive," I said.

"In that case," Anita suggested, " it would be helpful to create a scene with your suspect. Do something that would really bother her and reveal her deep-seated anger."

"Yeah, but first I'd have to identify the chief suspect. Right now, I have too many in mind."

***

A week later, Danny came to me with the idea of doing a virtual show. "Since the club is closed, it might be the only way to keep our customers," he said. "We have a solid list of phone numbers and email addresses. We can contact your loyal followers, Izzy, and ask them to join us. And we can do a little promotion on TV and a few newspaper ads. That is if you're willing to do it."

I was curious but a bit apprehensive. "I don't know, Danny. What's involved?"

"Nothing too difficult. You just do a set without an audience in the club. Instead, they'll be watching you on their computers. You'll be performing on stage."

"You mean I won't get their reaction? I won't know if they're laughing, or not?"

"If they have audio capability, you'll hear their reactions, including laughs. It's a new technology. What do you say?"

"Okay, Danny. Who said you can't teach an old dog new tricks? I'm game. Let's do it."

***

The following Saturday, I stood on the club stage without an audience, feeling stranger than I've ever felt in any venue. Only Danny and a handful of technicians were there. Besides Anita, who was home nursing a cold, I had no idea how many people were viewing at home. On a signal from Danny, I began my set.

People keep asking: "Is this virus really all that serious? Listen, the churches and casinos have closed." When heaven and hell agree on the same thing, it's pretty serious.

I placed a drink in each room of my house today and called it a pub crawl.

The virus has turned us all into dogs. We wander around the house looking for food. We get told "No!" if we get too close to strangers. We get really excited about going for walks and car rides.

I hope they give us two weeks' notice before sending us back out into the real world. I think we'll need the time to become ourselves again. And by "ourselves" I mean lose the ten pounds I gained, cut my hair, and stop drinking at 9 a.m.

I stepped on my scale this morning. It said: "Please practice social distancing. Only one person at a time on the scale."

Day 46: The garbage man placed an AA flyer on my recycle bin.

I reviewed my new monthly budget. Gas, zero

dollars. Entertainment, zero dollars. Clothes, zero dollars. Groceries and booze, 2,979 dollars.

I was in a long line at 7:45 this morning at the supermarket that opened at 8 o'clock for seniors only. A young man came up and tried to cut in front of the line, but an old lady beat him back with her cane. He returned and tried to cut in again, but an old man punched him in the gut and kicked him. As he approached a third time, he said: "If you people don't let me unlock the door, none of you will ever get to shop."

That's it, folks. You've been part of an experiment in show business. Hope you all tune in again next time.

Danny took the mike and thanked the unseen audience for joining our experiment. A technician, using a slit-throat gesture, signaled him that we were no longer live. I thought the gesture was appropriate since I felt we had all just died. Danny and the small group of technicians applauded in the empty club. Danny told me he would soon receive an audience report on how many people tuned in. He would let me know. I called Anita, expecting to be invited over. Instead, she said her cold left her tired and not in the mood for company.

"No problem, honey. Take two aspirin, gets lots of sleep and call me in the morning."

"Yes, Doctor."

TWENTY-ONE

THE NEXT MORNING, WHEN I hadn't heard from Anita by 10 o'clock, I called her. Almost immediately, I knew something was wrong. She didn't answer until the fourth ring. She seemed to have trouble speaking. Finally, I determined that her cold had developed into something more serious.

"I'm having trouble breathing," she said. "And I have a fever." Then she started coughing.

Suddenly, I recalled the many news reports that described the early symptoms of the virus that had swept the nation and the world. "I'm coming over to take you to the hospital," I told her.

"Oh, that's not necessary," she mumbled. "I'm sure it'll clear up."

For a very smart lady, I thought, that was not a very smart response. She's just being stubborn. "Please don't argue with me, honey. I'll be right over. Get dressed."

She was wearing tan slacks and a brown sweater and sitting in an armchair when I arrived. Her face was flushed. She looked tired. She held my arm as we walked to my car parked at the curb. Within fifteen minutes, we were in the emergency room at St. Joseph Hospital. About a dozen people sat in chairs, waiting to be treated. They wore face masks. I went to the desk and told an elderly woman that I had brought in someone who appeared to have the symptoms of the virus. My words didn't seem to have any impact until she looked at me.

"You're Izzy Brand, aren't you?"

"Yes, ma'am, can you help us?"

"I'm a regular fan of yours, Mr. Brand. My husband and I go to your shows at least once a month."

"Thank you. My friend is very sick. She has a fever. I think she should be admitted and isolated."

The elderly woman glanced at Anita, seated nearby, and then at the other people in the room. "Do you think she has the virus?"

"That's what I said," I snapped.

"I'll alert someone right away. Please take a seat."

Wearing a mask and gloves, a nurse arrived within minutes, took Anita's temperature, peered into her eyes, and placed her in a wheelchair. "I'm admitting her," she told me. "You should leave now." I leaned over to kiss Anita but the nurse stepped in front of me. "You need to distance yourself. Go home and stay there for at least a week. And wear a mask when you go out."

I watched the nurse wheel her out of the ER and disappear in the corridor. Suddenly, the virus was no longer suitable material for a comedy routine. My sweetheart was sick, very sick with a dangerous disease, and my world had turned upside down. I put my hand in my jacket and retrieved a small jewel box containing the ring I intended to offer her at exactly the right moment. She had put me off several times in the past, but I kept the box in my pocket. And now, as I watched her disappear down the corridor, I wondered if that moment would ever come. A feeling swept over me that I haven't felt since I learned of the death of my wife, Clara, and later my friend, Sam. It was a feeling of deep despair.

TWENTY-TWO

AFTER A RESTLESS NIGHT, I got out of bed at six o'clock and tried reading the newspaper but found it hard to concentrate. The news was mostly about the growing number of Americans admitted to hospitals across the country, including Colorado. Anita was one of those persons. I couldn't wait to see her. The clock in my kitchen told me it was still only 7:16 a.m. I couldn't visit Anita until nine. I wasn't hungry but I forced myself to eat a bowl of dry cereal and milk.

Danny called to tell he received the numbers on our virtual show Saturday night. "They were excellent," he said with excitement. "I think we should continue. You could probably attract a new audience, Izzy, people who've never seen or heard you before. Who knows where that could lead? What do you think?"

"That's nice," I mumbled.

"That's all you can say? That's *nice*. Is something wrong?"

"Anita's in the hospital. She's sick with the virus. I'm very worried about her."

"I'm sorry, Izzy. Is there anything I can do?"

"No, but thanks for offering. I'm going to the hospital in a little while to see how she's doing."

"Let me know, will you? The whole gang will want to know."

I assured him I'd call, hung up and sat in my recliner, staring at the clock. I remained there for almost an hour, my brain on a wild tour of memories, all of them involving Anita. Then I headed for my car, stopped, went back to my apartment, and put on the mask I had acquired the day before.

Why I didn't get stopped by a patrol car for speeding I'll never know because I was walking into the entrance of St. Joe's within fifteen minutes. At the desk, I inquired which room Anita was in. The middle-aged lady, probably a volunteer, scanned a directory and said: "Room 321. But you can't see her."

"Why not?" I asked with some impatience.

"She not permitted any visitors"

Again I asked, "why not?"

The woman looked at me with steady gaze. "You could ask the nurse at the station on her floor."

I thanked her and headed for the elevator. Within minutes I stood before a nurse. She wore a mask—as did all the nurses nearby.

"I'm here to see Anita Bender."

"Are you her husband?"

I'm often asked that and I hate having to say I'm not, just a friend, because I'm more than a friend. We're sweethearts. Have been for years. How do you say that to strangers? She has no family. I'm the person closest to her. I ignored her question. "How is she? Can you at least tell me that?"

"You'll have to ask the doctor. He's seeing her now, but he should be out in a few minutes. What is your name?"

I gave her my name and asked, "What's *his* name?"

"Dr. Barringer."

"I'll wait." I took a seat and glanced at my watch. It read 9:20 a.m. The mask on my face felt smothering. I lifted it off my nose and took a breath. *That's probably not a good idea. Defeats the purpose of the mask. But the air here should be clean of the virus, shouldn't it? The doc's name is Barringer. Sounds familiar. I hope he has something positive to say.*

Another ten minutes passed before the doctor arrived. I saw the nurse gesturing toward me and watched him approach.

"Mr. Brand, I'm Dr. Barringer. Anita tested positive for the virus. We're trying to reduce her temperature. She's having trouble breathing. It's called dyspnea, and it's very distressing for her. She needs a ventilator."

"Would that help her breathing?"

"Yes, if we can locate one."

TWENTY-THREE

WHAT DO YOU MEAN 'if you can locate one?'"
I asked the doctor. "Isn't a ventilator
standard equipment in a hospital?"

"It's normal to keep a certain number on hand,
but this pandemic is not normal. We've run out
of ventilators, and we're having trouble finding
more. The state was promised a shipment from
the feds—they have a supply—but our order has
been set aside. I don't know why, but I think it's
political."

"Political? That's unconscionable when people's
lives are at stake."

"I agree. Thank goodness we have ample
supplies of other PPEs, like facial masks, gloves
and gowns."

"But what are you doing about ventilators?"

"We're contacting known suppliers—anywhere
in the world. We'll find some. We just don't know
when."

I noticed that my fists had involuntarily clenched
and my jaw felt tight. "In the meanwhile patients

like my friend are at risk, is that right?" I said.

Dr. Barringer looked at me with a blank expression. "I'm afraid that's true," he muttered, and looked away. "We're doing the best we can," he said as he left.

I stood at the nurses' station, immobilized, not knowing what to do. Down the hall, my loving companion lay gravely ill, dependant on medical help that itself was frustrated by a lack of necessary equipment. Dr. Barringer was hoping to locate ventilators somewhere in the world, but had no idea when that might happen. I had to do something! But what?

Barringer. The name sounded familiar. I'd heard it recently, but where? And then it came to me. I reached into my jacket pocket and retrieved the little notebook I started carrying since I got involved in the Mervin Gardens murders. I flipped some pages until I came to the list of victims. There it was.

Died May 2. Dr. Russell Barringer, age 82. Widower and resident six years. The coroner's report said he died of a heart attack.

However, the autopsy ordered by Carlos revealed

the presence of ethylene glycol, Carlos told me. It had caused Barringer's kidney to fail—and his heart. I wondered if the victim was related to Dr. Andrew Barringer.

I left the hospital and slipped behind the wheel of my car, my mind again on Anita. An idea had begun to form. The name Larry Slater had surfaced. He was the former Marine that Anita and I met recently at the Brooklyn Deli. A recent widower. Nice guy. Owned a small manufacturing plant making medical supplies. Did he make ventilators? I checked my cell and found his number listed under Contacts. I left a message with his secretary.

"Please ask him to call me as soon as possible," I told her. "It's an emergency."

***

Back home, I slumped into my recliner, George in my lap, and stared out the window. From where I sat I could see much of the Rocky Mountains called the Front Range—all the way from Pike's Peak on the south to Mt. Evans due west and to Longs Peak on the north. That's more than a hundred miles between Pike's Peak and

Longs Peak. Even though it was still spring, the peaks were covered with snow. A great view. The weather, the mountains and plains, the generally laid-back disposition of most people, and the fact that Denver was home to four professional sports teams, all created a desirable to place to live. Between Aspen and Denver was a hot bed of comedy. Sometimes I felt like living in Colorado was like living in a bubble that protected me from the ills and troubles of the world.

"'Tis A Privilege to Live in Colorado," the *Denver Post* formerly proclaimed every day on its editorial page. I couldn't agree more. Of all the places I've been around the world—Europe, Asia, Africa and South America —there were darn few that could pry me away from Colorado. For some reason the *Post* dropped that line and replaced it with "There is no hope for the satisfied man," words attributed to the paper's founder. I agree with the message, but I still miss the stuff about living in Colorado being a privilege. As far as living in a bubble, that was true until the virus came along and suddenly the bubble was no longer any protection.

My thoughts were interrupted by my ringing

cell. It was Larry Slater, returning my call.

I got right to the point and told him about Anita needing a ventilator. "Do you make those things?" I asked anxiously.

"I'm afraid not, Izzy. I only make small items, but I know a guy who does manufacture them. Let me check with him."

"I don't want to sound pushy, Larry, but this is urgent."

"You bet it is," he agreed. "Anita is a wonderful woman. I'm right on top of it. I'll find a ventilator for her, Izzy. You can count on it."

***

Assured that vital help was on the way to treat Anita's dangerous condition, I allowed myself to ponder the murders at Mervin Gardens. It had been two weeks since they first came to my attention, and it was time to wrap up the investigation.

I pulled my notebook out of my pocket and began scanning the pages. I wanted to focus on the most likely women I thought might be the killer. Of the eighteen women on my list, I quickly eliminated about ten based on my research. Five of them were reliant on walkers to get around. I crossed off three more on hunches. I was down to five. I assigned a number to each of the five to indicate their likelihood of being the killer. Besides living in Leah's building, the one thing they had in common was each had demonstrated a clear tendency to anger easily and ferociously. I had collected examples. Scuttlebutt told me some had difficult childhoods, others lousy marriages. I guessed all had inherited crummy genes. All had traits and characteristics associated with serial killers.

Number 5 was Elena Pulasky. She was the youngest and the most nimble so she could have easily outrun me that night at my club. She'd had arguments with all the victims, but nothing came of them, I was told.

I assigned Number 4 to Dorothy Spelt. She also had disputes, some of them loud and threatening. I'd heard whispers about her obnoxious behavior.

Number 3 was Ida Sanders. Normally a quiet woman, she had surprised her neighbors with violent outbreaks of anger that frightened them.

A very strong candidate for Number 2 was Olive Ogilvy. Never married and a bit of a hermit, she had gained a reputation for challenging her neighbors on a score of matters, sometimes going so far as threatening them. Some feared her.

That left Number 1. In my gut, I felt I knew the killer. The evidence pointing to her was overwhelming. One problem, though. She was handicapped, confined to a wheelchair. How could she have executed all those poisonings under the circumstances, and how could she have run away from me at the club? I had started thinking about her as a prime suspect at Sidney's funeral. She had described how they shared wine. Later, I learned she had served wine while entertaining all the other victims. Was it at those social occasions that she shared more than wine—that she laced the wine with some form of poison? But the most striking piece of information I learned about her came from her college transcript which Carlos had obtained. In her senior year at the University of Kansas, she had studied toxicology and was a very good student. He'd also learned that she was abandoned as a baby by her mother. Had she suffered a traumatic childhood? It was another characteristic of serial killers.

Of all the suspects, she was the most self-assured. She seemed to think that she was smarter than the police and, certainly, me. In her mind, she probably was convinced she would never be linked to the murders. It would speed things up, I thought, if I could find a way to have her incriminate herself.

***

I made myself a light snack of tuna on a few crackers and a glass of milk, and then took a nap.

When I awoke about twenty-minutes later, I decided to go back to the hospital to check on Anita. Although I was not allowed into her room, the nurse permitted me to view her through a glass window. She was awake, propped against a pillow that allowed her to see me. She generated a weak smile and raised a hand in a feeble greeting. I waved back and mouthed "I love you." She put a hand to her heart.

Dr. Barringer arrived, nodded to me and the nurse, and entered her room. He scanned the chart on a computer near her bed, and then placed a stethoscope on her chest. I could see them conversing while he asked questions and she responded. After a while, he came out of the room and approached me.

"We've got her fever down , but she's still coughing and having trouble breathing. She told me she had recently consulted with a client who just returned from China. I'm pretty certain that's how she got infected." He said he would have his staff contact the woman and try to trace her other contacts.

I told him about my call to Larry Slater.

"If he can locate a ventilator for us, that would make all the difference in the world."

I said, "He promised he'd call and let me know. By the way, are you related to Dr. Russell Barringer? He lived in Mervin Gardens."

"Yes, he was my father. Did you know him?"

"No, but I know he was one of several people living there who recently passed away. I'm sorry for your loss."

"Thank you. Coincidentally, I just received a call from a police detective. He said he was investigating those deaths as homicides. He said my father—and the others—were all poisoned. He said you were assisting the investigation."

"Yes, Anita has a friend who lives at Mervin Gardens who also lost a close friend. Did your father ever mention anyone living there who threatened him?"

"No, but he told me he had an encounter with a neighbor that upset him."

"Did he provide any details?"

Dr. Barringer thought for a moment, then said: "She confronted him one day in the hallway— she lived next door—and accused him of always playing music too loud. He liked opera and had a collection of disks he often listened to. He apologized and said he would reduce the volume thereafter, but she continued to rant at him until he walked away from her. From previous encounters, he was convinced that she was mentally unstable, probably seriously paranoid. As a retired psychiatrist, he recognized her symptoms."

"Did he tell you her name?"

"No, I don't think so. But he said he felt compassion for her because she was also handicapped."

"In what way?"

"He didn't know, but she was confined to a wheelchair."

TWENTY-FOUR

SITTING IN MY CAR outside the hospital, I pondered my next move. Dr. Barrringer's comments convinced me that I absolutely knew who killed his father, Leah's lover, and the others. After a few minutes, I made a decision.

I drove to Mervin Gardens and rang the apartment of Mrs. Margrette Tripp. I identified myself and after a moment of hesitation, she buzzed me in. I walked through the lobby door to her first floor apartment. Her door was slightly ajar. Seated in her wheel chair, she looked at me with a bemused expression, blended with a hint of anxiety.

"May I come in, Mrs. Tripp?"

She produced a broad smile. "Of course, Mr. Brand. What a pleasure!" I was impressed with her ability to alter her demeanor on a moment's notice. I walked into her living room and stood momentarily until she invited me to sit. I seated myself in a comfortable-looking armchair with an ottoman. She continued to smile as she watched me, warily. The smile never left her face.

I said, "You know that I'm assisting the Denver police who are investigating the deaths here at Mervin Gardens. May I ask you a few questions?"

"I've already talked to the police, but I'll be happy to answer your questions, Mr. Brand."

Again, I marveled at her manufactured politeness.

"May I get you something while we talk?" she asked.

It was exactly what I was hoping she'd say. "Coffee would be nice," I replied.

"I'll just be a minute." From the kitchen, she said: "What would you like to ask me, Mr. Brand?"

I wanted to see her expressions when I posed my questions. "It can wait until you join me, Mrs. Tripp." My plan was to say something that would trigger her anger.

After a few minutes she returned with a tray on her lap containing a cup of coffee and small glass of cream. "Please help yourself," she said, placing the tray on a table in front of me. "Now, what would you like to know?"

"The coffee seems a bit hot," I said. "I'll wait until it cools off."

"I'm sorry. I guess I overheated it. So how can I help you?"

"Could I trouble you for some sugar? I have an insatiable sweet tooth."

"I understand. I like an occasional sweet once in a while, too. I'll be right back."

As soon as she was out of sight, I removed a thin flask from my jacket pocket, unscrewed the lid, and poured a small amount of coffee into the flask, and then quickly slipped the flask back into my jacket. I glanced at the cup. It looked undisturbed, except that the level of coffee was inconspicuously lower. I hoped Mrs. Tripp would not notice. A potted plant and an expensive-looking vase caught my attention nearby.

When she returned, I asked: "I was wondering what you thought of Mrs. Sanders' comments at Mr. Luft's funeral. She seemed upset that he appeared ungrateful for her help decorating his home."

"Oh, that woman," she said. "She had a difficult childhood. Lost her mother when she was a child and apparently never got over it. I have no sympathy for her. I lost my own mother when I was two years old, but I never let it dictate my life. You've got to learn how to overcome life's challenges."

I put two teaspoons in my cup, stirred it vigorously, and quickly resumed our conversation. "You have a lovely apartment. May I take a better look of your view?"

She looked at me suspiciously. "The view is best from those bay windows in the corner, although there's not much to see."

I picked up the coffee cup from the tray, stood, and walked to the bay windows to study the steady stream of traffic. "I see what you mean. It's a busy street." I put the coffee cup to my lips, pretending to drink. I studied some photos on the wall. "Was that your husband?" I asked. "That handsome man in front of the fountain?"

"Yes, that's Dalton. We were in Rome."

"I see a hotel in the background. It looks familiar. Were you near the Coliseum?"

She rolled her wheelchair to the wall to get a closer look at the photo. I grabbed the chance to pour my coffee into the potted plant. Then I picked up the vase.

"You are correct," she said, peering at the photo. "I forgot the name of the hotel." She turned to face me, and saw me handling the vase. Her expression changed. "Mr. Brand, you didn't come here to have an idle chat." The tone of her voice was different, too. "Be careful with that vase. Put it down now!" The manufactured politeness was gone, replaced by unmistakable impatience and uncontrolled anger. "What's on your mind?"

"Murder, Mrs. Tripp," I said crisply. "Premeditated, cold-blooded murder. Thank you for your time. I can see myself out."

I left the empty cup on the tray, my flask securely deposited in my pocket and departed, but not before catching a fleeting glimpse of her. She sat on the front edge of her wheelchair, trembling with rage, appearing as if she would spring from the chair at any moment.

From the Mervin Gardens complex, I drove immediately to the Denver PD headquarters and raced as fast as I could up the stairs to Detective Carlos Collins' desk. Fortunately, he was seated there, poring over a file of papers. I stood in front him and pulled my flask from my jacket pocket.

"I don't know what the occasion is, Izzy, but you know I can't drink on the job."

"I need you to get this analyzed, Carlos. If it is what I think it is, we'll have reason to celebrate later."

***

A half-hour later, I pulled into a parking stall outside St. Joseph's Hospital. I took the elevator to Anita's floor, the third, and raced to the nurse's station. The middle-aged volunteer behind the desk greeted me with a smile. "Hello, Mr. Brand. Good news today. Your friend, Mr. Slater, just left. He delivered a ventilator to us, and Dr. Barringer has ordered it activated. Your friend is already connected."

TWENTY-FIVE

URING THE NEXT FIVE days, I made daily visits to the hospital. Anita remained in bed in the intensive care unit, looking pale and listless but, fortunately, her temperature was almost down to normal. With a ventilator affixed over her nose and mouth, she was breathing without discomfort. Her appetite was better. She was eating some solid food, and keeping it down.

"She's recovering," Dr. Barringer assured me. "She had a close call, but she's doing much better now. The ventilator was a godsend. I don't know how you found it, but you get a gold medal for doing it. She caught a break. The ventilator is the non-invasive kind, meaning we didn't have to put any tubes down her throat. This one is much more comfortable. And it's doing the job."

"When can I go in her room?"

"She's still contagious so that's out of the question. Let's wait a little longer, maybe another week or so. You can continue to visit her through the glass window."

Then, one day, she was moved to another room—without a window, and the only explanation I was given was that the room she vacated in the ICU was needed for a sicker patient. Not being able to see her was agonizing. I had to do something. I had an idea, but I had to wait until she was well enough to get off her bed.

Her new room was on the second floor and overlooked the parking area. When she was able to get off the ventilator and bed and sit in a chair, I called her and asked if she could have the chair positioned near the window. Soon she was looking down at me in the parking lot. I brought a pair of binoculars, focused on her window, and was able to clearly see her face, even behind the window screen. I felt like I was sitting in the room right next to her. My heart leapt. On the second day, I brought a lawn chair and set it up under a small tree that offered shade. We visited for almost two hours.

I kept up that routine for another week, talking to her on our cell phones, watching her through my binoculars. Color had returned to her face. She'd had her hair cut and styled and wore a touch of lipstick. She was beautiful. We regaled each other with funny memories. Time sped by like a gig at my club on Saturday nights. Anita got stronger.

At the end of the week, Carlos came by and brought a gorgeous bouquet of flowers.

"I've got something for you, too, Izzy. Your hunch paid off. The lab's analysis of your coffee showed it contained arsenic. Lovely old Mrs. Tripp tried to poison you."

With my mind on Anita's condition for two weeks, I'd almost forgotten about the Mervin Gardens murders and my search for a serial killer. "Now you can charge her with attempted murder. How about those other deaths?"

"We have enough evidence to charge her with all five murders. I'm going to arrest her now. Do you want to come along?"

"Absolutely. This I've got to see."

About twenty minutes later, I followed Carlos and two uniformed officers into Mrs. Tripp's apartment. She sat stiffly in her wheelchair, looking astonished at the thought that ordinary people may have seen through her meticulous planning and discovered her crimes. In the following minutes, the officers found supplies of arsenic, glycol, ricin and foxglove in her kitchen cabinet, tucked behind boxes of oatmeal and dry cereals.

I studied the poisons for a moment. "Peculiar alternatives for milk to go with cereal," I muttered aloud.

In a bedroom closet the officers found a black hoodie. Carlos displayed it in front of me. "How about it, Izzy, does it look familiar?"

I recalled the night I spotted someone leaving my club in a hoodie, and then sprinting away from me. Hardly someone confined to a wheelchair. Mrs. Tripp sat immobilized in her chair, watching her ruse fall apart piece by piece.

I spotted the vase that she claimed was valued at over a thousand dollars. I picked it up and tossed it playfully in the air.

"Stop that!" she screamed and bolted from the wheelchair as she hurtled toward me to catch the vase falling into my hands.

"I guess you don't really need that chair, do you Mrs. Tripp?"

"She's been cheating Medicare for years," Carlos

said, "long after she recovered from a broken hip years ago. We also found this." He handed me a journal. "She kept meticulous notes about everyone who offended her. The names match her victims. And she described how she poisoned each of them after inviting them over for wine, except for Mrs. Morgan, who didn't drink. So she was forced to drown her in the pool."

"Stand up!" he ordered, then thrust her arms behind her and snapped handcuffs on her wrists. "You're under arrest, Mrs. Tripp, for the murder of five of your neighbors and the attempted murder of Mr. Brand. Let's go."

I watched him and the two officers march her out the building while her neighbors looked on in astonishment.

***

That evening, while walking George, I ran into a friend. "Did you hear that Larry Slater's wife passed away?" he asked.

"No, I didn't know. How's he doing?"

"Nobody knows. He's disappeared, and we can't find him."

TWENTY-SIX

AFTER TWO MORE WEEKS in the hospital, Anita was discharged and wheeled to my car while a team of doctors, nurses and other hospital staff cheered. At her apartment, we sat in her living room and held hands. Leah Lamont joined us. She wore a mask and kept a discreet distance. It was heart-warming to hear laughter again, and to see a smile on my sweetheart's face.

Carlos was there too, also in a mask. "That was pretty imaginative of you, Izzy, to set that trap for Mrs. Tripp. Everything had to go just right—her leaving the room so you could grab a sample of the coffee, and your pouring the rest of the coffee into the potted plant. Pretty slick for an amateur dick."

"A trap for Tripp and a critique in rhyme," I said. "How poetic! What more can I ask for?"

Carlos turned to Anita. "And you deserve credit for suggesting we check out Margrette's mental health history. We had to get a court order, but we learned about her previous treatments for

232

paranoia and her stay at a private institution."

Anita said, "Her paranoia made her exaggerate minor disagreements. Her anger was out of proportion to the situation. It led to her determination to poison people."

"Exactly," I said. "She had a minor altercation with all five, but in her disturbed mind it was enough to justify killing them."

"I was able to track the episodes that marked her victims," I said. "Her journal entries confirmed everything. But even before that, when she told me she'd lost her mother at an early age, that clinched it for me. Many serial killers never overcame the trauma of being separated from their mothers."

"She even described how she got Sidney to inhale the ricin mist," Carlos said. "She pretended to see some flying insects and sprayed around Sidney's head. Because of the pandemic, she was wearing a mask and was protected. Sidney was not wearing a mask and was exposed to the ricin."

"I can't believe she put all this in writing," I said.

Anita said, "It illustrates how confident she was that she would never be found out. Moreover, she probably wanted to use the journal to relive her murderous adventures. She is a very disturbed woman."

"She'll need a need a good lawyer and a sympathetic judge," Carlos said with a tone of solemnity I rarely heard him express. Carlos has become philosophical, I thought, or is he just more worldly?

"If convicted," he concluded, "she'll probably remain in jail for the rest of her life. Another time she would have been executed. But Colorado has eliminated the death penalty."

"She shouldn't go to jail," Anita said. "She should be confined to a mental institution for the criminally insane, a place where she can get psychiatric help. Although, realistically," she added, "she's not likely to be cured."

That evening, Mrs. Tripp's arrest was the lead story on the late TV news. Reporters interviewed several relatives of the victims who credited me with cracking the case. TV also reported that the body of an elderly Denver man was found in Sloan's Lake earlier in the day. Based on a note found in the man's home, Denver police attributed the death to a suicide. He was identified as Lawrence Slater, owner of a medical supply firm in Commerce City. Police said he'd been despondent after the loss of his wife.

***

The following Saturday, Danny and the staff assembled at the club for another virtual show.

With one such gig under my belt, I was a lot more comfortable as I faced the camera for the second time. Anita sat at one of the tables with Leah Lamont. Danny introduced me as a veteran comic well on my way to a new career in cyberspace.

We're all in cyberspace, I began. *"What a world we're living in today. Right? Introverts love it. Extroverts are going out of their minds. A friend of mind installed mirrors on every wall in his house so he'd always have company.*

You know what hasn't changed? Blonde jokes.

A blonde walks into a doctor's office with both of her ears burned.

"What happened?" asks the doctor.

"I was ironing my blouse and the phone rang. I picked up the iron instead of the phone."

"That explains one ear, but what about the

other?"

"The jerk called again."

A ventriloquist is performing with his dummy on his lap. He's telling a dumb blonde joke when a young platinum-haired beauty jumps to her feet. "What gives you the right to stereotype blondes that way?" she demands. "What does hair color have to do with my worth as a human being?"

Flustered, the ventriloquist begins to stammer an apology.

"You keep out of this!" she yells. "I'm talking to that little jerk on your knee."

True story: When my late wife and I were first married, we took a small apartment in a three-story building. We both worked, but I left home a bit earlier than my bride. Shortly after moving in, I was confronted by an attractive young blonde on the first floor landing. Standing just outside her open door, she said, "Excuse me, sir, would you mind zipping me up?"

I complied and she thanked me. This went on daily for a full week before I told my wife about it.

The next morning, she followed me down the

stairs but stopped halfway down. The blonde appeared on the landing, turned around, and displayed her bare back to me. "Would you, please?" she purred.

Just then my wife came down the stairs and said, "Here, dearie, let me help you with that."

It was the last time I was asked to zip up my neighbor's dress. But my wife wanted to know why I waited a whole week to tell her.

Without an audience to see, I had no idea what the demographics were. My club audiences usually included a sizeable number of seniors, so I assumed they were represented tonight, comfortably seated in their living rooms. Time for a joke they could relate to.

An elderly couple goes to a fast-food place for a quick meal. The gentlemen orders a single hamburger, fries and a drink. When it's ready, they find a table and he begins to eat. A truck driver, seated nearby, notices and offers to buy the woman her own meal.

"That's okay," she says, "we share everything."

A few minutes later, the trucker observes that the wife still hasn't taken a bite. Again, he offers to buy her a meal.

"She'll eat," the husband assures him. "We share everything."

Unconvinced, the trucker asks the woman, "Why aren't you eating?"

"I'm waiting for the teeth."

An hour later, I wrapped up the show with this closer:

In surgery for a heart attack, a middle-age woman has a vision of God by her bedside. "Will I die?" she asks.

God says: "No, you have thirty more years to live."

With thirty years to look forward to, she decides to make the best of it. So, since she's already in the hospital, she gets a face lift, breast implants, liposuction, a tummy tuck, hair transplants, and collagen injections in her lips. She looks fabulous!

The day she's discharged, she leaves the hospital with a swagger, crosses the street, and is struck immediately by an ambulance and killed.

Up in heaven, she sees God. "You said I had thirty more years to live," she complains.

"It's true," says God.

"So what happened?"

God shrugs. "I didn't recognize you."

The show over, Anita and I left for her place. We sat side-by-side on her sofa, my arms around her.

"My niece left me a message," I told her. "Seems Malcolm's boyfriend was dying of AIDs. Malcolm moved in with him to comfort him. He apologized and asked her to forgive him. He agreed to a divorce."

"Now they can go on with their lives," Anita said. "They'll both be happier."

And now that Anita has recovered, she and I will be happier, too, I thought. I couldn't take my eyes off her face. Being able to hold her again almost made me shudder with joy.

"What's wrong, Izzy?"

"Nothing. Why?"

"There's a tear in your eye."

I wiped it away and said, "I was thinking how sick you were and how close we were to losing you." She squeezed my hand and kissed me. "You are the sweetest man in the world, my darling. I love you."

It was exactly the moment I'd been waiting for. I reached inside my pocket and removed the little jeweler's box.

THE END

Acknowledgments

Hearty thanks to Marilynn Reeves and Dennis Knight for their thoughtful comments and to Michael Allegretto for his critique and wise suggestions. His insightful observations made a profound difference in the final version.

Author's Note

Inspiration for this book came from my surroundings and my neighbors and friends. We live in a complex of buildings set aside for older folks, those over fifty-five. There are lots of amenities, beautifully landscaped grounds and the frequent sound of sirens. Ambulances are called regularly to attend the occupants who require a trip to the hospital. Some never return.

In the hot days of summer, my friends hang around the outdoor pool. They tell stories and, knowing that I write mysteries, ask me what I'm currently writing. Several months ago I told them I'm writing about a serial killer in an old folks community similar to ours. They wanted to know if they were in the book. Of course, I told them, but well-disguised. No one in the book represents a real character. The people I've literally invented are composites of people. The serial killer in the book stands alone—she is simply a figment of my imagination and represents none of my neighbors.

The coronavirus pandemic arrived after I started the book, and affected everyone I knew in one way or another. Of course, I had to put it in the book as part of the plot. The pandemic was still among us as this book was being published. Although one occupant contracted the disease and died, none of my friends, fortunately, have been affected to date.

CPSIA information can be obtained
at www.ICGtesting.com
Printed in the USA
LVHW041046180322
713721LV00004B/331

9 798679 666320